Advance praise for

THIS ROAD WILL TAKE US
CLOSER TO THE MOON

Praise for

THE DISTANCE BETWEEN

*This writer's territory, the cauldron of the family, and its
ultimate good humor, reminded me of the work of Anne Tyler,
Elizabeth Berg, and dare I say it, Alice Munro. Wry, witty and
touching, this book is a joy to read.*

Madeleine Blais

*A novel both funny and sad. A fresh new voice in American
fiction, a voice of impressive range.*

Tracy Kidder

*Some passages in this novel recall the furious intensity of Allen
Ginsberg's "Kaddish," while other sections are reminiscent of
the subtle, lyrical gifts of T.S. Eliot's "Love song of J.Alfred
Prufrock." One cannot help but hear poems in this prose, and
like Eliot and Ginsberg, this writer tackles timeless issues.*

Book Page

*So precise is the writer's touch you want to listen until she has
no more to say.*

Martha McPhee

The road novel for mothers, surprising, sad, hilarious, and true.

Alix Kates Shulman

In language that is spare but enlivened with flashes of purely joyful writing, this author has the gift of revealing the commonplace in the most uncommon of ways and brings new insights into concepts we all thought we completely understood.

Booklist

Heavily interior in its center of gravity, intelligent and moving.

Kirkus Reviews

A keen observer of gestures and detailed interpreter of loaded silences, dissecting domestic relations, creating sharply drawn, quirky yet familiar female characters struggling to learn from the contradictions of their lives.

Publishers' Weekly

THIS ROAD WILL
TAKE US CLOSER
TO THE MOON

Also by
Linda McCullough Moore

The Distance Between

written as eliza osborne

THIS ROAD WILL TAKE US CLOSER TO THE MOON

Stories

Linda McCullough Moore

"That's a Fact" first appeared in *The Saint Ann's Review;* "Is Anyone All Right?" in *Relief;* "Mother's Helper" and "Ball Doll" in *The Queen's Quarterly;* "The Next Life" in *The Southern Review;* "Walking by the Rectory" in *Chrysalis Reader;* "Four Kinds of People," *in Room Magazine;* and "Final Dispositions," "This Road Will Take us Closer to the Moon," (as "Rejoice and Be Glad"), "Incidents and Dreams," "My Country 'Tis of Thee," and "Freeing Spirits" in *The Sun.* "Final Dispositions" appeared in *PUSHCART PRIZE XXXV.*

In loving memory of

Irene Osborn Moore

TABLE OF CONTENTS

THAT'S A FACT

IT'S 1955, THE DEAD CENTER OF DECEMBER, and we're sitting on a shabby sofa in a second floor apartment of two German people we don't know. They have just finished feeding us strange sausages and cabbage, noodle pudding and mean-crusted sourdough, and finally, rock-hard anise cookies I saw my brother spit into his handkerchief.

Now here we sit: my mother, and my father, and my sister, and my brother, and the Germans, who it would appear have used up all their English over dinner. They smile and gesture and use German words to tell about their Christmas tree whose every branch holds upright lighted candles, which surely must have burned and flickered through the shabby parlor all the while we sat and ate or pushed odd foods around our Melmac dinner plates. This tree, this whole apartment, might have gone up in flames; we might be three charred children now, no longer bored or chilly, sleepy, ready to go home, but burnt to bone and ashes— singed and smoldering—frightening even to smoke-seasoned firemen.

The Germans jab their fingers, point at a gray tin pail of water sitting near the tree.

"For the fire," the husband says.

My mother nods and tugs her skirts to cover more cold leg. My sister coughs and says, "Excuse me."

We don't go to other people's houses much. I'm not sure why we're here tonight or, for that matter, why the Germans are here either. My brother's *Weekly Reader* says they're building a new Germany. So why didn't they stay home?

The husband switches on the radio.

"*Rockin' around the Christmas tree in a swingin' song tonight.*"

He turns the knob.

"*And Molly and me, and Baby makes three, we're happy in my [ba-dum-ba-dum-ba] blue [ba-dum-ba-dum-ba] heaven.*"

He turns it off. The silence in the room is louder than it was before.

"This is no music," the husband says in spitty English. "In Germany there is the music."

My mother smiles. My father exhales. Out loud. It sounds like he has been collecting air inside of him all night.

The wife jumps up and hurries from the room and comes back with a hard black cake, and we each take a piece. I want to tear off bits of mine to roll into sticky balls to pelt the candles on the tree. I want the tree to catch on fire and the husband to throw water everywhere and the wife to scream and run around. And then I want to go home.

We had a contest at our school. Whoever read the most books won a prize. The day it was announced I raced Tommy Graff to the public library right after school. I read books like a crazy person and I won. *THE STORY OF D-DAY*. That was what they gave me. A boy's book. They'd thought Tommy Graff would win—even though everybody in the whole school knows he skims.

I read the D-Day book. You do when it's a prize. It said the Germans were bad people—even their generals, especially them. It said at Normandy they shot our soldiers in the face.

"In America there such opportunity." The wife is trying to be friendly; she's telling us, please don't feel bad my husband doesn't like your music on the radio. "It is so good," she says. "Our son, you see, can make $8 working in one day, and to do this seven days each week, and my Philip too to work with sciences and we will have a house maybe in one year from now in Buffalo."

"It must be hard to come from Germany." My mother's probably been working on that sentence for the last half hour.

"Oh no," the wife says. "Oh no, this is not hard. The war, the war is hard, but now to be living it is easy, and to come to America."

I want to tell her this is not America, this is Marksville, Ohio. America is California and New York City and Louisiana. America is what you read about in school.

"I am scientist at university," the husband says. "The world will open for us now."

"Well, good for you, buddy." My father's voice could knock down soldiers. "I didn't finish high school." He addresses his remarks to the shoelace he pulls between two fingers. "And let me tell you, my friend, your life is pretty rotten when you got no education in this country, and a wife and three kids and a fourth one on the way."

I snap my head around to catch my mother's eye, but she is looking at her lap. My sister grimaces, and shrugs *don't look at me, I didn't do it.*

I can't believe there are going to be more people in our family. My mother said three was plenty. More than plenty. She used to say that two was fine.

"What we have here is a recipe for failure." My father's whisper says *you pay attention.*

The Germans look all pleasant and expectant, as though this too is some good thing in America, if they could only figure out what it might be.

"This country is possible for everything," the wife says. She's working hard.

"Maybe for you." My father switches back and forth from pathos to mean anger so fast it makes a person's head spin. "Just let me tell you what it looks like from the other side, my friend." My father puts both feet on the floor and leans forward. "I make 40 bucks a week, plus commission if I ever sell a car, and this time of year I can assure you no one's even stopping by to waste my time. I go in every morning, six days a week, and scrape the snow off eighty cars and go inside and sit with my coat on for thirteen hours till they close up and send us home. My gas bill is close to $60, I owe the doctors $34, electric is $6.50, the broken stove will cost me $8, the food bill at Henry's is $47, the furnace will be $30 if it's a dime. I still owe $11.50 for snow tires, and the dentist's hammering me for $15, and that, my friend, comes out of the $40 I take home Saturday night."

I want to think the Germans are befuddled, mystified. I want to think their fractured English has deserted them. But I know better. This sort of recitation must be the same in every language that there is.

The tension stirs a phantom breeze; the candles on the Christmas tree give scary flickers. They are the only things alive inside this room. The Germans sit leaden. They had such hopes for the evening. They have such hopes for America.

I read a story in the newspaper about a family in Germany who were so poor they ate candle wax. You won't find that in the *Weekly Reader*. The paper said that family died of poisoning. They boiled green needles from a yew tree to make broth.

People in a family need to be so careful. My family are. Everything—our whole life up till now—has been possible because we're careful. We keep it all inside our house. Whenever we go outside in the street, we take our different selves, and leave real life at home. Until tonight.

But still I know this is no sudden thing: my father spilling his guts to these German strangers. He has dragged himself, inches at a time, over to the cliff's edge and, head heavy, tumbled over. That is how it's done. A person doesn't run a mile to reach the edge and hurl himself into the void that ends in jagged rock below, for the simple reason that by the time you've reached the edge, you're winded, and you stop just shy to catch your breath and reconsider. The ones who take the plunge make camp just crawling distance from the edge and every day inch closer, living in a place where tumbling over—be it suicide or saying all—is not a great departure from routine.

A lifetime after this disaster night, I will, one morning, realize that I have tiptoed, crept, and sidled close up to that edge more often than I care to think. At cocktail parties, while other people struggle to craft careful conversation, I blink, twice, and see a woman frown in my direction, and I wonder: Have I blurted out, "Things are so bad with us we may divorce tonight" or have I only stood there, awkward, stricken silent. In time, the saying and the holding back confuse and fuse until finally they are very much the same. It's only what I am that is my mother jerks me back each time, does not allow my leaping.

The Germans have surrendered to bewilderment. They did not come to America to hear my father say all this beside their dangerous Christmas tree.

The husband reaches out and pulls the water bucket closer to his chair. The wife points to the cake. In accusation? Some desperate hostess offer of distraction?

But no, oh no, we will not be diverted, not from our lives. We'll take them home with us and sleep with them tonight. We children will grow up and carry them away and keep them with us everywhere we go.

And then the years will sneak by while we've got our backs turned. And forty Christmases will pass, and my sister will call me up late on a Tuesday night to tell me this will be her fiftieth Christmas with our parents, and I will say, "Do you remember a night when we were little when Dad told some German people all our troubles, and they had real candles on their Christmas tree?"

"Frederick _____-_____." My sister says a name I do not catch, all consonants, too many syllables. A harsh-sounding name. "He's still in town," she says. "Berte, his wife, is dead. He teaches at the college. He worked with van Brown on rockets in Germany."

"Von Braun," I say. "This guy was a Nazi? Did Dad know that? Half of Dad's friends from high school were killed in World War II."

"Nobody in town knew about the rocket business for years," my sister says. "He got into a lot of drugs in the 70's. He thought he was a hippie. He started saying he worked in Germany on a project to develop the atomic bomb."

"But you *do* remember the night I'm talking about?" I say.

"Sure. Dad let it all hang out. He used to do that. He told us once at supper that he killed a man. Nobody was talking about killing people or anything related. He just said it. He got that creepy look and said, 'I killed a man.' It had me scared for years."

"Dad was in an accident," I say. "A car crash. The other driver died. I'm surprised you were old enough to remember that Christmas, though."

"Oh yeah. Frederick stood there all night holding a bucket of water beside the Christmas tree. They had hung potatoes wrapped in tin foil to stabilize each branch that held a candle. They could have burned the house down." My sister does this little cough she does. "We could have all gone up in flames." She coughs again. "We were lucky."

Then she tells me she's put a little something in the mail for me for Christmas. Nothing big, she says, but she hopes I'll like it. And we hang up.

I lean back and look up at the ceiling. You carry something in your head a certain way for forty years, and then one night your sister calls you on the telephone and says, "He tried to make an atom bomb." And all the old facts—all the sad, little, family facts—need to shimmy over, move out of the way to make room. And new facts plop down on their big rear ends and knock the old facts on the floor.

Adolph Hitler never got the atom bomb. That's a fact. They wrote it in the *Weekly Reader*, in the book, THE STORY OF D-DAY. And—a lesser-known fact perhaps, not written anywhere—my family once spent an evening with one of the men who did not make that bomb.

And that's the way it goes. Our little lives, our stories we imagine so unusual and sad, take place right next door to other people's stories. We spill our guts to strangers—with little children sitting by—or we move to America and put up flaming Christmas trees and never hint a whisper; we sell cars or teach physics at the junior college; we swill Maalox or smoke pot and call ourselves a hippie or a victim. Gather seven different people in a dark December living room—*be careful not to bump the tree*—let some of them live two blocks over for three generations in a row, let some of them cross oceans to be new somewhere, have the small ones be the shyest children in the world.

They, every blessed one of them, will have a story.

FOUR KINDS OF PEOPLE

I'M SITTING IN THE LATE AFTERNOON OF MY EXISTENCE at Logan Airport reading the fine print on the backside of my boarding pass when my life walks in. Well, one of my lives, my former life. Carlton. He doesn't see me—not exactly a first in my experience—as he trails a brown-haired woman and two boys to the four empty seats directly across from me, oblivious as ever. I stare at the wife—for so she must surely be—and think she is some version of the woman I would have become had I stayed married to Carlton, borne his children and these twenty years of quotidian perplexity in his surly company. She digs around inside her bag and pulls out an asthma inhaler she hands to a boy perhaps as old as ten or twelve, and it is as though I am being given a close-up look at what my life might have been had I stayed on Path A. Carlton still hasn't looked over in my direction, so I have not a clue if I am recognizable in my current incarnation. He looks up. I catch his eye. He frowns as he was ever wont to do and makes a sudden urgent business of studying his shoes. The wife—I'll call her Mary Ann—asks him how long the layover in Charlotte is. He asks her how the hell would he know. Still the charmer. He looks at me again, a look made up of equal parts of menace and imploring.

What is his scowl asking? I don't know how long the layover in Charlotte is. He gives his head the slightest shake. It's very subtle for a lawyer. Ah, he's asking me to please not say hello, not smile, shake hands, and introduce myself to Mary Ann. It's clear as day. If we had been able to communicate half this well in Ithaca, we might never have gotten a divorce. He doesn't want the wife to know it's me, for reasons I will in all likelihood die not knowing. I lift my shoulders and my eyebrows and my open palms. The wife looks up. I make quick circles with my wrists and raise and lower my eyebrows and scrunch up and unscrunch my lips. Carlton sighs like he has just been stabbed and stands and tells his wife he's going to get a paper. Once he's behind her he motions with his head for me to follow.

I don't think so.

"Do you know anything about the weather in Charlotte?" I ask Wife Number Two and smile at the bent heads of the two boys wired to the game gadgets in their hands.

She shakes her head no. She seems disappointed. "I never know the weather," she says.

"That's okay," I say. She really does seem bummed out about it. "I mean, it's not like the weather really matters."

"But then what does matter?" she says.

Oh dear. Clinical depression. I feel guilty. I mean, if I had stayed with Carlton, she never would have married him, and she'd be off somewhere this evening not giving a fig that she can't handle the weather channel.

"I'm sorry," she says and gives a rueful smile.

"No," I say. "I'm sorry. I am." When I was making out my list of pros and cons for leaving Carlton, it never once occurred to me I might be loosing the furies on some other woman's life.

"I'm just tired," she says. "We just flew in from London, and we have two more short flights. It would have been faster to walk."

I went to London with Carlton once. He had a lot of family there. They picked us up in a miniature mini, four people in a car the size of a six-pack. We toured all over, took the Flying Scotsman overnight to Edinburgh, saw the big military tattoo, and went down and met his mother's cousins in Snowdonia. It was someplace near the Irish Sea where I first got the idea of leaving Carlton.

"England is so nice," I tell the wife. "Travel is great for giving a person new ideas."

I'm fishing.

"I don't know about that. We just go to visit family. The houses are too small to think in."

"I know," I say.

"Are you going to Charlotte or going on from there?" she says.

"I'm on my way to meet a thousand priests in Myrtle Beach."

"Are you a nun?" She looks nervous. I bet nuns get that a lot.

"Nope," I say. "It's about the only job I haven't tried. But then I'm not dead yet."

I try to think if you can be a nun if you're not still a virgin, which is I think a pretty big part of the whole nun thing. I look up and see Carlton standing not ten feet away. Eavesdropping. The sex I had with him surely wouldn't likely bar me from the convent life. It was so un-carnal. So pure. So soft and warm and safe and gentle. Carlton was a bastard out of bed, but sex with him was the kindest sex I've ever known.

"This is my husband," the wife says as he sits down.

"Ummm," I say instead of hello.

"Where's the paper?" she says to him.

"What paper?" he snaps back.

Maybe Mary Ann and I could go be nuns together.

I smile at Carlton. He thinks that I have blown his cover, but he's hoping against hope. He sits stony-faced just on the off chance. He knows Mary Ann and I could grind him down to powder.

"Are these your boys?" I say to Mary Ann.

No, we rented them for the trip. I make up the only interesting reply.

"Umm," she says, but makes no great show of interest.

"I'm going to get a paper," Carlton says and walks away.

"He sure does get a lot of papers," I say to Mary Ann.

"Are you married?" she asks me.

"Not at the moment, but I have high hopes for the thousand priests at Myrtle Beach."

"Oh," she says as though she has some clue what that might mean. I start to explain, but then think better of it. There are about four people in the world who are interested in the difference between Catholic and Episcopalian priests and their matrimonial proclivities.

"And you're not a nun, you say."

"Nope, still not a nun." I can see why she has a little trouble with the weather channel.

"I was just reading," I say to her, "about how people start new lives, how they just reinvent themselves and start the whole thing over."

"I'm really tired," she says.

I get it. I was exhausted all the time when Carlton and I were man and wife, and I was only twenty-four.

I look over and I swear she's crying.

"I didn't mean reinvent yourself tonight," I say. "I know you're tired tonight, but when you're rested. Think about it."

"Think about what?" Carlton plops down. He's clearly had a couple shots of something smelly.

"Mary Ann is just tired," I say.

"Who's Mary Ann?" they say together.

I look beyond them and see a pudgy guy in a tight, knitted cap bend over to take something from his suitcase. His chinos come nowhere near his waist, and on the broad elastic of his underwear in bold black letters is printed BOXER JOE< BOXER JOE< BOXER…

There are really three kinds of people: people who get married and sit in airports bored out of their minds together, or people who sign up with the Mother Church and be priests and nuns and things, and people who are out there all alone and wear signs on their underpants and most nights drink a lot of beer.

No, there are four kinds. People married to each other, or to the church, or to their single selves, or people who sit alone in airports late at night inventing lives for strangers they will never see again, but people who, when the boarding starts, stand up and straighten out a jacket, gather up their gear, and do not rule out the possibility, not ever, that they are starting on a journey that might take them to some place where no one's ever been before.

THIS ROAD WILL TAKE US CLOSER TO THE MOON

Warning: This document contains information about how the story ends.

Don't read it if you haven't gone back home to have Thanksgiving with your family.

Wednesday night
9:32 p.m.

"Hi, It's Margaret. From Match.com." I'm whispering into the phone in my mother's kitchen, volume and timidity leftover from high school, thirty-two years and two husbands ago. I've been home three hours and already I'm looking for a way out.

"I can't hear you," a man's voice says.

I can hear him clear as a bell.

"It's Margaret," I say. I use my stop-traffic voice. "From Match.com."

I sound like I'm calling 911.

"Oh hi. Say, can I call you back? I'm in the car. I'm with my kids. They're home for Thanksgiving. Can I call tonight around 10?"

"No," I say. "Everyone will be asleep. Everyone is practically asleep right now. I'll call you back another time."

I hang up feeling rejected by all the inhabitants of the known world.

10:30 p.m.

I stand in the dim light of the kitchen with my mother eying the miniature turkey she bought today. "Just in case everyone is sick tomorrow and we can't make it to the restaurant for Thanksgiving," she says. "I hate restaurants."

My mother went to bed at 8:30. Now she's up again.

"Do you think this turkey would feed thirteen people?" my mother says.

It's the size of a large pigeon.

There's noise out front, and two young nieces burst into the kitchen, followed by their dad, my brother Ned, who ducks as he walks into the room, though his height hardly warrants the nod. His wife Hannah and their two teenage boys follow, weighted down with what appears to be all their earthly possessions.

"Sorry we're late," Ned says. "The car caught on fire."

He always has some excuse.

11:15 p.m.

"Hello. Hello?"

"Hi, it's me again, Margaret. From Match.com."

Hi. it's me from your geometry class, from church, from college…. I was your roommate for four years. Your first wife.

"I know who you are. I'm so happy you called. I thought you said you'd be asleep."

"I am."

"Well, I'm glad you called."

Thursday

7:23 a.m.

I, who never rise before everybody else on the planet is up and dressed and has accomplished two important things—I, who usually start the day one down—am clothed and caffeinated, cloaked and out the door before any of the family have begun to dream the dreams that ring the borderland of consciousness. I, who stood in the pantry in the peaked light of dawn, just as long ago my father must have stood on chilly mornings, all alone… my father, dead these twenty years.

It's cold outside, in the way that makes a person feel resourceful, the air that crisp and clear. I've got the whole town to myself, the only person in ten neighborhoods out and about on this Thanksgiving morning. The Pilgrims won't be grateful for another seven hours; no NFL tight end's tendon will tear till hours after that.

I round the corner by Fred Boyd's house. "Red Fred" we called him, for uninspired reasons. I turn onto Washington Avenue, and walking toward me is a little boy, third-grader size, with a ceramic mug in one hand and a jar of Coffee-mate in the other. He's wearing soft-looking flannel pajamas. I can't make out the pattern, but in the spitting mist, he looks entirely warm and right.

"Morning," I say. "Where you off to?"

"I'm going to my grandmother's house," he says. "We always have breakfast together on Thanksgiving." He, who has only been alive for seven Thanksgivings, eight at most, he, who has I hope been drinking coffee far fewer years than that.

"Could I go with you?" I say.

"Sorry," he says. "If it wasn't Thanksgiving...."

"No, no. I just meant, could I walk you there?"

"I can't think why you couldn't." He points out his destination four houses over.

"How's your life?" I say. It's a question I usually wait to ask people, one I work up to, but his grandmother lives right here. There isn't time to ask what grade he's in and does he like school—a sorry-ass question in the best of circumstances.

"My life is good," he says. "I have my own room now. They moved my sister to the attic. My turtle died, but he was ready to go. I'm going to go ice fishing with my dad. We're going to wait till the pond freezes. And today is Thanksgiving, and I'm going to have coffee with my grandma."

I stand and watch him walk up the pathway but turn away quickly as he frees one hand, just before he opens the front door.

8:07 a.m.

I walk into my mother's house to find the whole family buzzing about Brian, the teenage hooligan next door. It seems last night he braked to take a sharp turn on wet leaves—that counterfeit of ice—and smashed into the guardrail, totaling his mother's car.

11:32 a.m.

My father long lamented that his life had amounted to nothing. I think of this refrain as my two stunning nephews, fruit of the fruit of his loins, sit singing hymns in careful harmony. My absent brother has a son who's off in seminary and a daughter who's a hospice nurse. And at the table in the dining room two golden girls with braided hair and plastic-sandaled feet are choosing real live ducks and pigs and goats, school books, inoculations, from the Save The Children catalog, a splurge they saved up for all year.

Let God decide whose life amounts to nothing.

12:32 p.m.

We park the car, and I walk with my two nephews toward the nursing home.

"Take me out and shoot me, but don't you ever let your parents put me in a place like this," I say.

We walk into the vaulted-ceilinged room for visitors in the Day Villa Manor where we have come to see our Aunt Mary. She's ninety-three and only lately here herself. She fell and broke her hip, the ticket of admission.

The rest of the family are already in attendance, my sister holding forth. I notice that my mother's hearing is much better here. At home, she's practically stone deaf. I whisper a swear under my breath. She frowns and shakes her head at me.

Ned spots a piano over in the corner. He signals to Hannah, who sits down on the bench and starts to play. We sing. It's easier than shouting inane questions at our aunt.

We sing hymns, all five verses, the words burnished on our brains back when we had no say in the matter: "Just As I Am without One Plea." "The Old Rugged Cross." The Silbermans in matching wheelchairs in the corner mark the beat.

"Do you know 'Hava Nagila'?" I ask Hannah. She can play anything.

"Hum a few bars," she says, and she is playing with me by the third line.

Ned jumps to his feet and grabs my mother, who stands planted as he swirls around her. The kids all join the dance. My mother starts a goyish stomp. The Silbermans are beaming.

"'Hava Nagila'?" My sister frowns. There is nothing she cannot disapprove of—just so long as it was my idea.

1:45 p.m.

We all comb our hair and shave or put on lipstick, and then head out to the country club for turkey. We take six cars. No one in our family thinks anyone else in the family is safe to ride with.

I'm not saying anyone is wrong.

The place is on the bleak side, but the food is magnificent. The gravy is worth the trip the Pilgrims made. In steerage. My sister says they make it from beef drippings. She lives one town over, so I figure she knows. We have all begun to eat when my niece Patricia stage-whispers in her dad's ear. "I have to puke."

"Hannah," my brother says, and mother and daughter run from the room.

"I'll take her home," Hannah says, running back in and grabbing her coat.

"Happy Thanksgiving," my mother calls over her shoulder, takes another bite.

2:30 p.m.

I see two fat people pass down the buffet line heaping stuffing and mashed potatoes into two of those lidded Styrofoam boxes, so I go ask if takeout is available. It is. $17.95 per box, and no one but God will know if you stuff the entire thing with turkey or with mincemeat pie. I go tell Ned he should take a dinner home for Hannah. "$17.95," I say.

"No," he says. "She won't want it."

Well, of course she will, unless she's eaten herself senseless on tea and toast at home.

"She will, " I say. "I'm getting two to go so we'll have leftovers at home, but you should get her one. She'll want it."

He says no four times.

4:56 p.m.

I gather up a carload of nieces and nephews for the ride home from dinner, and once they are belted in, I drive them to the cemetery where our people have been buried for the past two hundred years: Taylors and Mackensies. The oldest nephew whips out a fancy camera and runs around in the now-fading light, taking pictures of rocks and trees and tombstones. I take a peek at his camera's little screen. The stones in his photographs all read "Macintosh," not "Mackenzie." He has a hundred pictures of the wrong dead family. If they were daguerreotypes or Kodak color prints, he would be required to figure out what to make of that. As it is, he hits DELETE.

This isn't right. It should not be so easy to delete the photographs you take. It should be costly, wasteful. You should hesitate to rip them up, and then only after you have saved them twenty years and come across them in a bureau drawer and studied them awhile, wondering, and trying to remember.

It's almost dark. I get the children in the car, and we head back to town.

"Aunt Margaret, turn here. Turn right," Molly, my little niece, pipes up from the back seat. "Turn right."

"Why, honey?" I slow the car and hit the turn signal. I'm a big fan of sudden inspiration. I make the turn.

"Thanks!" she says. "This road will take us closer to the moon."

5:06 p.m.

At home Hannah says she's eaten scrambled eggs and Raisin Bran.

"I told Ned to bring you a meal," I say. I slip the Styrofoam containers of roast beef gravy slathered on four pounds of turkey and mashed potatoes into the back reaches of the fridge. Later I'll steal cold nibbles when nobody's in the kitchen. I'll be damned if Ned will get any.

By evening I'm offering heated samples to the children, then to my mother and my sister, but everyone says no; they're sending out for dinner because Ned wants ribs.

Ribs.

6:40 p.m.

Hooligan Brian next door has been saying all day that the car crash happened just before eleven last night, but now it seems that it was really 4 a.m., and he can't tell the police because he was driving after junior curfew. Ned goes over next door to make him go to the police and confess. We have been beating confessions out of people for generations out of mind. Our ancestors were Covenanters in Scotland in the 1700s who swore oaths not to eat until they'd murdered every English Christian who dared disagree with their incipient-Presbyterian theology. There is no record that one of them died fasting.

8:45 p.m.

"What happens to this house when mother dies?" I ask Ned. He's younger than I am; he doesn't know how high the stakes are. We have finished surfing every channel on the new TV my sister hoped would tame the winds and waters of our mother's long descent. "What will happen to the house?" I ask my brother again, as though he had been assigned the deciding. My older brother would scowl and tell me that I never loved our mother. My sister would tell me that I'm being morbid, a dismissal she's been using since the day she learned the word in junior high school. *Morbid* and *maudlin.* That's what vocabulary words are for: to distance you from other people.

"Sell it," Ned says. "We would sell the house. I could use the money, with four kids to put through college." As though this house, where I was brought home as a baby, might be offered in the marketplace. I don't tell him, but though I live twelve states away I'd thought we would be keeping it so that when I come back to visit no one still living, I could stand and look out the back kitchen window and see the scene my father saw beyond the shadows every morning just before he headed off to work at 4 a.m.

"I always thought we'd keep the house," I say.

"Who would live here?"

Dad, I don't say.

Nor do I say that maybe I will buy it from the siblings and tear it down and build a tiny, oddly situated park, or give it so some poor young family, who might raise four other children here.

9:30 p.m.

We just heard the police came to arrest Brian next door. Turns out it was not a guardrail but a house he hit.

11:16 p.m.

"Hey, it's me," I say. We've moved from Match.com to this in one day's time.

"Hey, how are you? I called you earlier. Your mother answered. She called me 'sir.' I don't think she likes me."

At least he's not stupid.

"Say, could you call me tomorrow night on my cell?" he says. "I'm driving to a party then, and we could talk on the way. I told my friends I'd met somebody. They all want to meet you."

"Don't *you* want to meet me first?"

******

A person can move lockstep through the hours of a day, but it can take a while for life to tie up all the pieces.

I once read a list of probabilities. It said the chances of a person knowing in advance where and when and what kind of catastrophe will befall him is 1 in 112 million. It also said the chance of nothing major and terrible happening to you or your family or your friends in one calendar year is nil.

My mother's house will be struck by lightning in a couple of years. It was struck once before, back in 1969. Lightning *does* strike the same place twice. Make a note. The house will burn to the ground. No phoenix from the ashes this time.

The children will grow up—except, that is, for the little boy walking in the misty rain in his pajamas, carrying the Coffee-mate. He will be buried by his grandmother a week before his eleventh birthday.

Brian the outlaw next door will die in his bed when he is old, when he is very old.

I will end up almost marrying the Match.com-met man, but will think better of it in the end. I will not regret my decision. And I will.

And later, years from now, my brother Ned will say *Remember that Thanksgiving? Everything was perfect.* He will be referring to this Thanksgiving with its car accidents and nursing homes and cemeteries and families and turkey and mashed potatoes—like the batch in the Styrofoam container that will be discovered in the far back reaches of the fridge near Christmas, a little green, and very dry.

You don't know anything is happening while it is going on. You can stop the clock a hundred times a day, but when you wake up the next morning, it will still be 7:45 and there will be an odd tapping on the roof, and you'll be late before you've even gotten out of bed.

******

Friday
The day after Thanksgiving
7:04 a.m.

The phone rings. I answer. No hello, just "Margaret, tell Mum to come up to Wal-Mart parking lot to give me a jump-start. The car is dead."

It's Ned. He expects our mother, at the age of eighty-seven, to hop into her little Mercury before she's had her oatmeal and her Lipitor and come to rescue him. A natural consequence, I like to think, of serving her son breakfast in bed every single morning for all four years of high school. (Let the record show that this same woman claimed she had no interest whatsoever in getting up to watch me eat a piece of toast—this when I weighed ninety-four pounds soaking wet and walked two miles to school in sleet and rain and snow. Et cetera, et cetera.)

"My car is dead," Ned says again, in case I had forgotten, which I sort of had.

"Of course, it's dead," I say. Ned's car caught fire driving here on Wednesday out on Route 80. As his wife tells the story, first came smoke from beneath the hood, then flames, and children jumping from the car. The fire burned itself out in a matter of a few, wild minutes. "I'm pretty sure that's fixed it," Ned said, and got the kids back in and drove two more hours to Mom's house.

Right. An electrical fire in the engine corrected the problem. This is what comes of growing up in our family: a person thinking that a good fire sets things right.

I figure even in a car that didn't have a very recent engine fire, car trouble's what you get for going shopping at 4 a.m., which Ned and Hannah and three of their four children did.

"It's your favorite," I say and hand the receiver to my mother.

8:00 a.m.

Everyone is packing up and leaving. Brian, the home wrecker from next door, is out on bail, and my brother Ned has decided to take him home with his family to New Jersey.

"I can't think prison is very likely to improve his personality," Ned says, and tells Brian to duck down in the back seat on the way out of town.

It is the sort of thing that people in my family do. My mother slips a thin roll of dollar bills into Brian's hand. "In case you get thirsty on the way," she says.

8:47 a.m.

I'm zooming down Route 80 going eighty-seven miles an hour. It doesn't seem that fast. I glance over as I pass a car. A 1960 Buick. It's a maroon color they don't make anymore, a maroon they never should have made in the first place. I look more closely, and there he is: my dad. He's driving and my mother is complaining at his side. At any moment she could slide in his direction, or the skinny children in the back seat—I their chief—might go flying over the front seat if my father hit the brakes. No worry. He hardly ever brakes. We are safe as houses. The whole family is headed for the beach. We'll have to drive all day to cross the whole of Pennsylvania and the barren southern strip of New Jersey. We won't get to the darkened rooming house till after nine, but there will be a breeze coming from the unscreened windows in the upstairs bedrooms. It will lift the curtains. It will tell you even in the dark, the ocean is not two blocks away. And those children will hear the sound of waves upon the beach and smell salt air at unexpected moments off and on down through the years.

I step on the gas and pass the car, and I start humming, "Hava nagila. Hava nagila. Hava nagila."

Hey. Hey. Hey.

11:37 p.m.

Everyone in the world is asleep but me. I forgot to call the Match.com man. I'll call him in the morning, move on to that phase. I check my email, then look up *Hava nagila* on Google. *Hava nagila,* it means "Let us rejoice and be glad."

Hey isn't even Hebrew. It's Burmese. Also Finnish, Mandarin, Greek, German, Latin, and Dutch. *Hey* means "Well, goodness gracious, mercy sakes alive, will you look at that!" And it means "Enough!" And "Look at me!" And "What a surprise! I never would have seen that coming ... not in a million years." Or, in country dance, *hey* is "a choreographic figure, in which the dancers move in an out amongst each other, circling, touching, moving far apart, then moving back to touch again."

INCIDENTS AND DREAMS

IT WAS A NIGHT OF INDUSTRY. All night long I was packing lunch boxes, making peanut butter sandwiches for children who will grow up to be somebody famous. Cutting off the crusts for Gertrude Stein, packing steak tartare for Charlie Manson—shaping fate—and pressing duck for Jane Austin, slicing cold wild boar for Gunga Din, and putting ketchup and cottage cheese in separate, little, sterilized containers with white labels for Richard Nixon. When I awaken I am polishing an apple for Dana Farber. So, there's cancer there. I don't know who Dana Farber is.

I roll over, open my eyes. Cancer. The bishop. The new bishop has cancer. Bone marrow. One in a hundred people who get cancer gets this kind; one in a hundred people who get this kind, gets the kind he's got. If they give him chemotherapy and radiation for five months, he has a 30 percent chance of a three-year remission. It seems when you get cancer, they load you up with numbers, like so many drug samples from your doctor, probabilities that make you wish you had paid closer attention in your statistics class.

I pull my several parts out of bed. In fifteen minutes I am packing lunch in real life and cooking real oatmeal. What would you give Ernest Hemingway for lunch? A fishing pole? A spear?

I would give Babe Ruth six candy bars for lunch. He was not a man held captive by his lipid count.

His wife says the bishop has started having fried eggs for breakfast, and sausages, and butter on his toast.

I am late for work. I am mostly always late, but not this late. I hate my job, and there is no way I can leave it till two weeks after I am dead, and even then I'll need a note from God. On the way to the office, I look at other drivers when I'm stopped at the light, on the lookout for a likely candidate to assume financial, emotional, psychological, and every other sort of support for me and my life to be. It's not exactly the fast track to remarriage, but at least it avoids the bar scene.

"You've got your review." My secretary speaks the words as though this were a thing a person might forget. Actually I had forgotten. "Mr. Peterson was looking for you a half hour ago."

I tap on Peterson's door lightly, hoping to make the sound soft and fluttering, as though a sparrow or a thrush beat gently, trying to get in. I've got birds on my brain. A certain demented robin has been hurling his full weight, all seven or eight ounces of himself, against the picture window above my kitchen sink. I can hear him, even from upstairs. The first time I heard him, I was afraid to come downstairs. It sounded like a burglar who was having trouble finding things. The robin hits against my window four or five times a day, but I need only to walk into the kitchen and he flies away.

"Ms. Mackenzie, please sit down." Peterson calls everybody "Ms.," except his wife. He calls her "the Missus." "Sit down, Ms. Mackenzie. I'm afraid I was expecting you some time ago."

"I'm sorry," I mumble. "Traffic, fire truck, accident, the road crew, detour."

"Yes. Well. Ms. Mackenzie, not to put too fine a point upon it, but I am afraid your work has been other than satisfactory. Babson says your creative work is strong, yes, yes, quite remarkable, in fact, but he finds you rather lacking in application. I am afraid this is really not the thing, really not the thing at all. What do you think?"

I think this man watches too much British television.

"I mean, what is it exactly that you can point to in the line of recent accomplishments?"

I packed Gandhi's lunch box, two tin thermoses of tap water and four grapes. I don't say it. I want my accomplishments to start standing on their own two feet.

"What do you have to show for your time? Where is your product?"

I see the row of lunch boxes lined up across his desk. "Oh, yes," I want to say, "and I spent three hours of my workday only yesterday sitting with a dying bishop."

I hardly know the bishop. I don't even call him by his first name. But his wife, Patty, had to go to Baltimore. She is a design consultant for the aquarium there, adept at the designs that keep the fish and water in one place. I had told her to call me for anything, so when she asked would I mind too awfully much sitting with the bishop until their teenage daughter got home from school, I said of course not.

"He gets pretty loopy sometimes with the sedatives they give him for the nausea," Patty said. "Unsteady on his pins."

He's doing chemotherapy at home. I always thought chemotherapy was done in hospitals with liquid chemicals and large, gray machines.

"Oh, but I forgot," Patty said. "You've got to work."

"No problem. Really," I said. "They hardly notice me when I am there."

Before I set out for the bishop's house, I put on earrings and more lipstick and my low, black boots—my only winter footwear, not counting fuzzy slippers and my serious snow boots. It seems fair to say that I am not a shoe person.

These leather boots are worn thin with scuffs in several places, so I grab a black magic marker and start coloring the worst spots in. The effort takes a good two winters off their age, but as I start on the second one I catch a glimpse of myself from the outside, and suddenly feel pathetic in some tawdry way.

I can afford to buy a pair of boots I don't have to ink in for special occasions. I can, but I don't.

"Come in. Come in." Patty greets me at the door. "You'll have to take your shoes off. Tom's a closet Buddhist."

At first I think she means he's in some trance state that my loud, shod footfalls might disturb, then I remember that the other Buddhists I know favor bare and stocking feet.

"I hope you brought a book," Patty says. "Tom will be working. Joan will be home from school at four. Come this way." She leads me to the paneled den. Her voice gets chipper. "The worst part of this entire disease is that it meant we had to buy a La-Z-Boy recliner. We held our coats up over our faces so no one would see us in the store. We were absolutely mortified. Ta-da."

She's pointing to the La-Z-Boy. She's also pointing to the bishop, who looks skimpy in the enormous chair. "Tom, this is Margaret. Margaret, this is Tom."

"In short, Ms. Mackenzie, I think we shall have to consider very carefully, very carefully indeed, to what extent and whether your continued association with Peterson and Bland Associates, in your current capacity, is in the best interests of the company or, in fact, yourself. Come. Come. You can't be happy here."

I look at the mole on Peterson's left earlobe. The first time I met him I thought it was an earring. I try to think when was the last time anybody wondered out loud whether I was happy. Does Peterson want me to be happy? Is it expected of me here?

"I'm happy you could come." The bishop's eyes are just as nice as in the pictures I have seen. "Nice of you to sit and watch me work." He speaks like a novice at this business of being sick, self-conscious, awkward in his role. He would probably feel more at ease in his decorated cone hat and heavy robes, with his tall shepherd's crook, standing in an Episcopal church somewhere, laying hands on bent heads, hands of confirmation, touching, just as he was touched by someone who was touched by someone who was touched and so on and so on back to St. Peter or Sir Thomas More— I never can remember which. In the l680s, two priests took a boat from Virginia back to England to have their heads touched in that way, then turned around and sailed back to America. They spent five-and-a-half months on a smelly boat on heaving seas so that the succession might remain intact, the line of bishops be unbroken. I look at this bishop in his La-Z-Boy and I imagine he would rather be fighting nausea on a swelling tide out in the middle of the Atlantic Ocean in 1687 than be sitting here with his wife's friend waiting to be sick.

"Well," Tom the Bishop says. That's what I call him in my mind. Just Tom is too familiar. Bishop Heminger is too high church. "Well," he says. "I guess this is it."

I'm not sure if he means his life or the arrangements for the slow part of the afternoon.

"Can I get you anything?" I say. "Coffee, tea, or something cold?" Whenever things threaten to get complicated, I start to offer liquids. I think a lot of people do.

"No, no, sit down. Please. Tell me something about yourself." He smiles with his tired eyes.

Well, I don't have cancer, or not that I know about is the first phrase that comes to mind. The words stop just short of utterance, and I smile back at him. I feel dopey and wordless, as though if I were to speak it would come out some hopeful gibberish. It seems so limiting that even in the face of death, we are bound to sit and struggle, stuff all of our accumulated sadness and puzzlement through the narrow funnel of old words, language, common speech and conversation, making do with the same words we have used everywhere for everything, just as, in the middle of his dying, this bishop must depend on La-Z-Boy recliners and Tums and Rolaids and his wife's new friends.

"I guess you know I'm sick," he says, and I'm relieved the spotlight is back on him.

"Mmm," I say. "Yes."

"I never figured on this," he says. "Not in a million years. I thought I would have a heart attack at eighty-eight at home in bed. I am not remarkable, and this is a remarkable disease. Extraordinary. But you don't want to hear this."

What to say? *Yes, I do. No, I don't.* I look at his eyes.

"I can't get over the surprise." He speaks and lifts himself to resettle his whole weight. He is still floppy looking in his big chair. "When I was a boy, my brother got TB. He was away at a sanatorium for eighteen months, and every day that he was gone, I was so healthy. All day, every day, I was so very healthy. For my mother. She needed it so much. I wasn't sick one time in a year and a half. I couldn't be. And ever after that I've been the healthy one, the one who never catches anything. And you know, the surprising thing is I was the one my mother loved the best. You would think it would be the other way around, that she would love the one who needed her. But no. I was the favorite son. I keep thinking she would be really pissed if she were alive to see me now."

I blink. I didn't know bishops said anyone was *pissed*, not even their dead mothers. But then it's not as though I've known that many bishops. Come to think of it, Tom is my first one.

"What your family thinks of you makes so much difference. My son Max is furious with me for getting sick. I feel like I let him down. And Patty, Patty continues to march unimpeded though all the forces of hell be arrayed against her. She is a formidable woman, dauntless—frightening, really, how strong she is. Even when she breaks down, she's tough. She breaks down into small rough nuggets." He takes a careful drink out of an oversized Pittsburgh Steelers mug, using a bent plastic straw. "I played the trumpet when I was in high school. I always wanted to play football, and instead I played trumpet in the marching band. It's funny how things like that still matter when you think you're coming up on dying. Did you want to play?"

He motions at my hands, and I realize I'm shuffling a deck of cards I have picked up from the table. "Oh, no," I say. "I don't even play cards really. It's just a nervous shuffle." I put the cards down and clasp my hands together in my lap.

"Do I make you nervous?" The bishop gives me a church smile.

"No. No," I say. "I'm always like this. I get relaxed about once a year."

"I've always been relaxed," he says.

"And healthy," I say.

"And healthy." He leans back in the chair and lets his eyes flutter shut. "Maybe I will sleep then."

"Oh, sure. Yes. Please do." I pick up a book from the end table beside me to show him how okay it is.

He sleeps for a long time, and I love the quiet of the afternoon, when everybody in the world is off and being busy.

It brings back a feeling I remember during my nephews' naps, a sense of being somehow outside of ordinary time and space. I flip through the book, which is all about how you can influence and control the vicissitudes of your immune system by what you think about and how you breathe and how much broccoli you eat. These books are fine, they make you feel like you have some control over what happens, so long as you don't stop to consider that if what they say is true—if you can make yourself well by thinking well-crafted thoughts—then maybe you're the one who made yourself sick in the first place. Small comfort there. I study the picture of the author on the back of the book jacket. She's wearing enough eye make-up to stimulate any number of immune system reactions.

The bishop blinks awake. "Lie down now," he says. He's all fogged over. "Lie down upstairs." He starts to get up and wobbles, and I take his arm and match his steps, and we two hobble like two eighty-seven-year olds across the slate floor, taking the single step up to the living room so thoughtfully, and then we are another age getting up the stairs. Once in the bedroom, the bishop falls across the bed, still holding tightly to my arm so that he pulls me down beside him. At first I think it's accidental, but he keeps his grasp firm as I try to rise. I look at him. His eyes are closed, and I think maybe he's in a lot of pain and holding on until the spasm passes.

"Be still," he says to me. It sounds like something from the Bible.

What's the Christian thing to do here? I know the bishop's bones are brittle. Patty told me he has broken two or three. The rest are fragile, thin and I think hollow. I don't want to go on lying here, but I'm nervous about moving. I don't want to break the bishop's bones. It occurs to me to wonder if all the saints in reliquaries in medieval rooms of large museums may have contracted multiple myeloma so that their bones would break into a multitude of splinters to be stored and venerated everywhere.

No matter. I am still lying here beside this man—he is still clutching my arm—and suddenly I want nothing in the world so much as to let go, relax, allow my full self, the weight and all of me, to be absorbed into the bed. To sink in, to fall finally into a deep sleep, into that surrender. Instead, I need to be getting up and out of here without doing any serious injury to the bishop.

He turns his face to mine. "Lie still," he says. "Just hold my hand." He's asking me to tie his shoes, to button up his coat and tie his scarf and kiss him on the cheek. To save his life.

"Dad. Dad." The bishop's teenage daughter Joan is standing in the doorway. "Dad." She's using an inflection adolescents use to speak to healthy parents.

"Oh." He struggles to sit up. I help him, and I give her a stupid, guilty smile.

"Your father told me he could feel something sharp sticking up through the blankets and the quilt," I say. "I can't feel anything." A four-word lie.

She turns away, disdainful. "You seem to think this interests me," she says.

She turns and goes back downstairs, leaving her scorn behind.

This girl will be a lifetime taking back the things she does today.

"What I am recommending is a new direction." Peterson pulls me back to him, gives my chain a nasty tug, jerking me back to Thursday morning, to his office, to my future. This will be the last day now before the first day of the rest of my life, I'm almost certain. "I'm thinking sales," Peterson says, feigning spontaneity. "Something about you says *sales* to me."

Sails, I think at first. *Red Sails in the Sunset.* But I know better. The man is saying *sales*, as in fire and going-out-of-business, as in death of a salesman.

There was a woman who lived on my street when I was growing up, a slight old woman, frail and bent. I can see her walk across her front porch, in her hand a bag of birdseed or a large metal watering can. Her house was a shade of green I have no name for, but the old woman was called Myrtle Carlson.

She had a son, a grown man, who lived with her. He puttered in the little flower bed that grew along the street side of the house, digging with an old, square-edged coal shovel and watering everything in sight, managing the floppy garden hose with jerks and tosses. A man living out his whole life in a single situation.

Then one day—it was the summer before I started junior high—a salesman came calling at the Carlson house. He came to our house first, but my mother drove him off with talk of Jesus and salvation, and her proffered Gospel tracts. We were not often troubled with repeat solicitations. I can see him walk away and climb the blistered gray steps to the front porch of the Carlson house, rapping on the flimsy green screen door, the old woman standing just inside, staring out of small, gray eyes that drooping lids and cataracts are closing down, pulling her thin sweater tighter, like the double layer of old Orlon might offer something like protection.

There she stands, confused by the shadow stranger, waiting with his sample case in silhouette, spot-lighted by the sun that warms his back. Say it is three o'clock. And the old woman's pasty-skinned, fat, pudgy son comes up the porch steps with his square coal shovel raised overhead, held out before him like a crucifer he brings down with a smart-sounding thud across the Fuller Brush man's head, striking him dead. And that afternoon the son, who had never been anywhere, went off to live in jail, and a week after that, his mother went off to live in heaven, a place she always had aspired to.

Change does not come easy. You want to tip your hat to anything that slits the seams of your life open, even just a sliver-width, to allow for the possibility of even minor rearrangement. You want to bow and curtsy, even if you cannot give the thing a name.

Sometimes, it takes a strong arm and a black coal shovel. Other days, no less than dynamite will do. It needed his impending death to make a bishop eat fried eggs, put butter on his toast, and offer up his old, familiar prayers to a stranger, petitions for salvation, or for mother comfort, that next best thing.

"Well, Ms. Mackensie?" Peterson is looking for the big answers here. "Well?"

"Actually," I say, "my reason for coming in today was to give you this." I open up my scuffed briefcase, rifle through the pantyhose and batteries and the granola bar, the headscarf and the Handi Wipes, and I grab a legal pad.

PLEASE ACCEPT MY RESIGNATION, I block print. YOURS TRULY, and I sign it, Margaret Mackensie, in a schoolgirl cursive. I rip out the page and fold it twice and hand it to Peterson, who unfolds it as though it were some invitation he has been hoping for.

"But why?" he says.

"What if I told you," I say, "that I was very sick. Cancer. The six-month kind."

"Well, are you sick?" he says.

I weigh and measure.

There are two women who, for the last handful of Sundays, have come to sit each week in front of me in church. They cling to one another through the hymns and prayers, caressing each other's heads and necks and arms during the early stages of the Eucharist. Not sexy touches really—more like comforting or soothing strokes—but anyway, I hate it. I sit and fret to myself, *How can they, in this heat?* And then last Sunday, during the Creed, right in the middle of the part about the resurrection of the body and the life of the world to come, the question came to me: *What if one of these two women is sick, very sick, dying? What of their caresses then?*

And I wonder, why do I, and everyone I know, require some dire disease to clear a little floor space for forgiveness, for forbearance of each other and ourselves? It takes such heavy life-and-death stuff to get us to lighten up. Why do we need catastrophe for definition, cancers and leukemia for clarity, for spelling the thing out: *You get one lifetime, and unlikely as it may appear, this is it, the one you get.*

"Well, are you?" Peterson says to me. "Are you sick?"

"No," I say. "No."

"Oh."

We are both disappointed. Neither one of us has got a clue about the big *What next?*

"So." Peterson moves his fingers around the edges of a stack of yellow message pads. And I wonder what medical diagnosis would I require to cut Peterson a little slack.

"So," I say, and I am standing up and offering him my hand, and before I know what has hit me, I am walking down the hall, my footfalls quick enough to make me look important, busy, late.

These things that happen to us—Peterson, my surprise retirement, my afternoon spent with a dying bishop—they are incidents. It is not reasonable to expect that they will change my life, but neither is it wise, I think, to rule out the possibility entirely. At any moment, when I least expect to, I might stop treating my life like a Wednesday matinee I got free tickets for. I might even strike up an old acquaintance-ship with tenderness, the kind the bishop had in mind, tenderness that's been away so long I had forgotten that it might just be off on some vacation, one that got stretched out way too long, one that was pure and perfect foolishness from the beginning.

IS ANYONE ALL RIGHT?

I WOULD KILL FOR A CUP OF COFFEE. I'm sitting in a movie theater beside a stranger—well a stranger to me—a man I met online, the single stupidest place to meet a person in the history of the world.

It gets worse.

The couple sitting in the row behind us met the same way, I'm almost certain. There are conversations people have when they first meet in person after days or weeks of email-fabricated flippancy and wild invention that resemble real-life conversation in no way.

"Do you have any hobbies?" my seatmate whispers, louder than is strictly speaking necessary.

"I have my own chain saw." These words spoken, as if in reply, in a husky woman's voice originating from directly behind me. I should have thought to move my lips, let her ventriloquize.

"I cut fifty cords of wood last year," her mate replies. A match made in heaven. They're both drunk, as far as I can tell—shared interests figure largely in online dating—and when the lights go down and I can turn around, I expect to see that they both resemble no one so much as one another.

"Do you have any hobbies?" my date asks in the same voice he used the first time.

"I don't think so," I say. It comes out sounding rude. Truth does that. A lot. But I'm not positive I do or don't. The only hobby that comes to mind is stamp collecting, which I don't, in any intentional way, and I'm afraid if I say yes, he'll ask me what my hobby is. I already have him pegged as someone who might well follow a fact back home to its burrow, and stand there, patient all night long if need be, until the truth comes up for air.

I'm pretty sure we two aren't soul mates. In fact, I'm not convinced we're slated to make it through the movie. I keep trying to figure how impolite it would be to leave him for a cup of coffee in the café across the street.

"I don't have any hobbies either." He sounds bereft. My first thought is to fix him up with the couple behind us. If he can't chop wood, surely he could learn to drink. I did once. Now that's a hobby. I unlearned it though. Now I just think of drinking, and I mainline caffeine and walk wired through life.

"Would you like to do something after the movie?" he says.

"Well, let's just see how late it goes," I say. I know full well it ends at 9:05. I always know beforehand when a thing will end.

The lights go down, the sound goes up; I feel a bass beat in my inner ear. The floor thumps.

"Stop that!" the chainsaw lady giggles and spills what smells like popcorn on my shoulders. "Oops, sorry about that, lady."

"No problem." I turn fully in my seat and face a child. She can't be more than twenty. Her match mate looks too old to remember much of forty.

My first impulse is to take her by the hand and lead her down the orange-lightbulb-lighted stairs, out of the dark, out into the summer evening.

"Fuck," she says. More giggles. "Oops, I didn't mean you." She buries her face in the man's jacket, and the laughing sounds like she is struggling to breathe.

"Would you like popcorn?" Bob—my seatmate, give him a name—asks me.

"I'm pretty sure I don't," I say, too equivocal once more.

"No thank you," I wax definitive, move from mean to stiff.

The screen is full of penguins, which I'm pretty sure I'm phobic of. I close my eyes and hope I've come to see some other movie. I thought it was about a plane crash and football, but I only skimmed the listing. I could have overlooked the penguin part. Once you're afraid, really afraid, of anything, it's everywhere you go.

A chirping comes from somewhere underneath my seat, and I lift both feet off the floor, eyes still closed, heart pumping. If there is one thing I fear more than penguins, it is things that chirp under people's seats in darkened theaters you thought were inhabited by nothing more harmful than lonely, online daters looking for love in all the wrong places.

The chirp again. I open my eyes and Bob appears to be frisking himself, then he extracts what can only be a cell phone from a jacket pocket and starts jabbing at it, making sounds I take for disgruntlement, but which may well be asthma.

The screen goes black and for a minute I think the movie's over, then as quickly remember that it hasn't started yet. Bob stuffs his cell phone somewhere, breathing more heavily than I find entirely appealing, and behind us the drunk lumberjacks between them manage to produce a sloshing sound like water in a large tank. It doesn't bear thinking.

Now we're on a football field, or the actors on the screen are. Bob and I and the match-made-in-heaven breathing down our necks are much as we have ever been and I think will ever be, playing on a field not half so level or well-marked, protected by neither helmets nor shoulder pads, clearly members of no team.

We already know from the previews that every player on the field will, before the popcorn's done, board an airplane, cheer in unison, drink Cokes, eat peanuts, and then die. And we know that after that will come the triumph of the human spirit. I hate the triumph of the human spirit. Especially because it so often follows a planeload of teenagers dying in a fiery crash.

And still we come to the movies. And still we sit and every time expect the show to end some other way.

"Are you all right?" Bob spit-whispers in my ear.

"Sure," I say.

"I just wondered," he says, and he starts his frisking thing again, though in response to no chirping sounds I hear, but then, the football game has gotten pretty rowdy; the cheerleaders, I think, overreaching—I mean, the team is Division III.

Bob fidgets with the buttons on his cell phone, which emits a blue light that's as offensive as a noise. The drunk woman behind us sighs in transport. I hear a Velcro ripping sound. The opposing team on the screen—many of whom will live to ripe, maybe overripe, old age—scores a touchdown. And one of the good guys lies on the muddy field, down for the count.

"Are you all right?" Bob asks again.

"I'm just going to go out and grab a coffee," I whisper. "I'll be right back."

"Shhhhhh," somebody whispers.

"Absolutely," I say out loud.

"Should I come with you?" Bob says.

"No," I say. "Stay here."

Somebody needs to man the phone.

I crawl over Bob, the long-life players make another touchdown, the chainsaw woman moans. I look back, but it's too dark to see if she is as naked as I imagine. I wave at Bob. He's patting his coat pocket.

Once outside, the air is fine. It's a good evening for football. I should go back in and rally everybody in the place to come outside and play a pickup game of flag—or tackle—ball. Someone surely has a football in his trunk. Or, for sure, he should.

Getting a cup of coffee takes approximately forever. There's a line and every coffee has six ingredients that have to be discussed in some detail.

I sneak my coffee back inside by pulling my arm up high in my sleeve until neither the cup nor my hand is visible. The hot liquid sloshes, dousing half my sleeve, and for the rest of what will be this querulous evening, every time I raise my arm I'll catch a whiff of stale caffeine.

"Are you all right?" Bob says as I slide past him.

"Humm," I hum.

"I thought you got arrested."

I try to conjure crimes of mine interesting enough to win the law's attention. But no. My crimes are sniveling and snipey, like my want of fellow feeling. My distain. There is no sentence to fit that crime. Unless you give the person life. That would do it.

"Who's that?" I say to Bob.

"The football coach," he says.

"I thought he was supposed to die in the plane crash."

"He was." Bob sounds put out. "But he decided to drive home, not fly."

There's always one.

"How's your coffee?"

"It's fine," I say. "I'm fine." Preemptive me.

And that's pretty much the movie. Moans and giggles from the lumberjacks, then something like a snore, Bob's periodic pat-downs of his pockets, cell phone, blue-light beams, football practice, human spirit sightings on the celluloid screen, punctuated by inquiries as to my well-being.

The coffee is good.

There will have been that.

But we're in the market for something more here. And so we get drunk and make out with strangers in modern movie multiplexes; people die, whole planeloads full; and we sit and fiddle with our phones and medicate ourselves with coffee beans.

"I'm sorry about the cell phone," Bob says as we each make a production of pulling on our sweaters once we're out in the lobby.

"Were you expecting a call?" I say.

"There's this guy," he says. "Well, I take him out for a meal on Sundays. He calls a lot to check on that. He's got early Alzheimer's. He isn't more than fifty. I used to do his dad's electrical work, then the dad died. I don't really know him very well. I just take him out to eat. He calls a lot."

"That's really nice of you to take him out," I tell Bob, and it is. *But you don't answer*, I want to say to him. *You check your phone in the movie, every time he calls, but you don't answer.*

That's the thing. Somebody takes us all out to dinner. Every Sunday. Because they used to do our dad's electrical work before he died. But they don't answer when we call them, I mean, not if they're in a movie. And we call and call, because we are never sure, or if we are we can't remember, just what it is we were to be expecting.

"Are you all right?' Bob says.

He's a nice man, he really is.

"Are you all right?" he says.

"Of course not," I say.

I'm giving him the only hopeful answer that I know.

I mean, imagine: this my life, I all right.

BALL DOLL

I FEEL LIKE I'M DYING, but I'm not exactly breaking new ground here. Someone in my family is always dying. My father, who *did* die a dozen years ago, used to say *People are dying who never died before.* Tonight, it's Aunt Mary, well technically, my sister Eileen's husband Tom's Aunt Mary, but close enough for our purposes.

We've just finished supper. Eileen has our mother on a three-day visit from the nursing home. I keep calling it parole. Each repetition of the word is good for one of Eileen's deep, long-suffering sighs. Tom's two twin sisters-in-law are here, and the four women are sitting in the living room. I'm *resting* in the next room, but I can hear their voices clear as day. It occurs to me to wonder is this what it's like when you are dead. You catch every word, you just can't answer back; people just don't know you're there.

"Aunt Mary's legs were swollen up like two balloons." Eileen's voice is schoolmarm taut. "She couldn't catch her breath, and when we took her to the E.R., they gave her morphine right away, and six different kinds of medicine, and I said to the doctor, 'Does this mean you're trying everything?' and he said, 'Yes.'"

The Aunt Mary in question is 97.

She looks older.

Ball Doll

I have a little scheme in mind. Tomorrow I want to take my mother back to visit the house where she grew up, the house where she never had a childhood—not a game, a doll, not a single playmate or a toy—the house I've never seen. It's only fifteen miles from here, my very own hometown, but oh, we are a family who for generations have been pushing the envelope on separation and distances between.

I tried to visit once a few years ago, but the daughter of the aunt who lives there now called up on the morning of the slated visit and said our coming would be too exciting for her mother's heart. Not "much excitement," as we used to say, but " too exciting."

I tune back in to the conversation that swirls around my ankles now, the water rising all around. It will require a clear head to navigate my tippy little boat through the whitewater that will be this visit with my sister, without smacking anybody with an oar or doing serious damage to my wee vessel.

"So after we took Aunt Mary to the E.R., Tom and I got our living wills made by a lawyer." Eileen, the consummate consumer, makes it sound a canny feat. "We also got long-term care insurance," Eileen says, as I imagine she eyes our mother with a certain meaning to her look. Eileen *is* our mother's long-term care insurance since mother had her stroke. Eileen tells me these two sisters-in-law give her a great deal of support, which from what I can tell consists of drinking copious amounts of rum and coke in Eileen's kitchen. I've always viewed these two women as the audience of the family—never players, at least not ones with speaking parts. I feel we might have dispensed with them at any time, but Tom's brothers will persist in staying married all their lives it seems. While my own two brothers shed spouses seasonally like some extra skin. I, little better.

The conversation moves from death to its precursors and accoutrements. No matter. We'll be back to death in no time.

The only place we will not go tonight is me. Conversation never wanders there. I have been waiting ever since my first visit home from college, freshman year, for someone in the family to say, "So. Margaret. How are you?" or, in some spoken way, to acknowledge my existence and the fact that I have been three states away, for weeks, for months, now suddenly, for thirty-seven years.

"So tell me about Brandon," one of the sisters says.

"Oh he's too young for long-term care insurance," Eileen says.

Brandon, Eileen's son, a man who throughout his late teens and early twenties devoted his life to following professional wrestlers on tour. A natural consequence, I like to think, of his having been exposed at a young age to one too many theme parks.

And what were we exposed to growing up, what set in stone our course in life? Our mother, probably. We were exposed to her.

If I leaned forward in my chair and craned my neck I could see the diminished vestige of that mother looking all but lost in Eileen's puffy, blue corduroy recliner. Oh, but that is not my mother there, gone wordless and deflated in senility. My mother is tempestuous action. She is speech. I hear her fifty years ago, enunciating so distinctly that her words are clear today:

"'This is the day which the Lord has made,' fashioned, by hand, out of scraps and pieces of old Saturdays and wasted Wednesday afternoons and His own well-practiced pretending. The gen-u-ine article, the real thing, a one-of-a-kind, never-seen-the-likes-of day, manufactured with more than just a little attention to particulars by God Almighty. I want you to think of that when you're in geography class today."

I'm not listening. I hear every word she says; I could repeat it back verbatim. But I'm not listening. I'm having a regular conversation—about milk money and homework, a debate about my rubbers or my boots, a conference to decide will it be raining when I walk home from school today—with the stodgy mother in my head. My mental mother, whose advice I always take.

The other mother is too tricky, too unwieldy for all practical purposes. A child requires a parent ordinary in some particular, in intention or design, hum-drum, boring, in at least a few details. A mother who creates herself anew every single morning of the week is a heavy burden for a child.

A child—myself, for instance—needs a mother who believes in recipes, who follows them religiously, from taking out the empty mixing bowls straight through till everybody's had enough, and maybe burped, politely, surreptitiously, and she has licked the serving spoon and covered what's left over with waxed paper or tinfoil. A child does not want a mother who loses interest in the printed word partway through the listing of ingredients and takes her inspiration from the far reaches of the back shelf of the fridge, premising a meal for several people—most of whom are only children—upon the discovery of a ancient jar of horseradish. You want for mothering a woman who does not, one time ever, dump mint jelly into the beef stew in the final hour of its oven life, then serve the vermilion meat on crinkly aluminum pie tins. Outside. After dark. For the change.

Life needs to be more regular than that.

Such school chums as I have are attracted to this mother of mine, seduced by her free fall through a day. It's fine if you are visiting; it is insupportable if it's your life. Girlfriends come over to do homework and stay for experimental, semi-permanent tattoos, or hair-straightening that will horrify their serious mothers when they go back to their lives.

These friends might stay and do acrylic colors on the living room wall, which my mother fully intends to paint the next day. A dozen years will pass, the colors fade, the edges smudge, but the design stay clear, the aberration as pronounced as the first day. My mother will declare the product *cheerful, heroic really, intelligent, a triumph over wallpaper and convention*. These girls' own mothers long since stripped refrigerators of their preschool art, while still it decorates the room where we might entertain, that is, if any grown-ups ever came to call.

There are grown-ups here at Eileen's tonight. In wild, or sedate, profusion; although, I think the only wild one may be me. It is as though my mother's stroke, in concert with Eileen, has sanitized my mother's personality; it's polyurethaned her life.

Eileen, a woman who has always done the usual things with slipcovers and jello, and these wives—these newcomers who only arrived after the fireworks were all done—the three of them together are now reinventing Mother in their image.

I wonder sometimes, is Eileen the mother, come to life, the one I long ago invented to save me from my life?

And I, have I become my worrisome, my oh-so-very real and fearsome mother?

Reality: it's not what you think.

Through all the years that we were growing up, in meanest fights, Eileen would lash out: *You're just like Mother.* That ancient taunt would have us rolling on the floor, pummeling the life out of one another, fighting like brothers. At some point the parents—for once, united on something—forbad the fights and so Eileen and I were stripped of spontaneity. We were reduced to fighting by appointment. *Meet me upstairs in five minutes. We can fight.*

It was never the same. Your heart has to be in it when you kill your sister. Like now. I don't hate her, I just actively repudiate everything about her and her family and her life. It has no thunder, just a familiar-feeling, weary irritation.

So am I? Become this crazy mother woman then? *I am* sometimes original the way she was. I could, probably, without too much paperwork, be granted a U.S. patent on myself.

It's early morning, that level playing field, the hour before anybody's reassembled, put back together at least enough to contemplate another day. Standing in the kitchen, Eileen, Mother, and I, making toast and steeping tea and searching for the marmalade, might well be three evenly matched contestants.

Nobody's dressed yet; we've not put on our differences. A man on horseback might think us much the same. The fact that no one speaks does much to perpetrate the illusion.

Seen at this hour, in this light, a person might think anyone of us might win. Another quarter of an hour, and the gods will be picking favorites.

They will, I think, not pick my mother.

Nor are they likely to be choosing me.

Eileen starts opening safety caps on several bottles, and my docile mother swallows far too many pills.

"You don't know what it's like," Eileen sighs. "To live here, day in and day out. Not when you come visit once a year."

Gentlemen, start your engines.

"I thought I'd take Mother to the farm today," I say, not in reply. "You want to come?"

"What farm?" Eileen says.

"Where she grew up."

"Oh, Margaret." The tone would be well suited had I proposed we have our mother drawn and quartered.

"Does that mean you're not coming then?" I say.

I raise my eyebrows at my mother. I can just imagine that she raises hers at me. I know such facial communication is no longer in her repertoire, but oh, it used to be.

At first, I liked this silent mother who came to take our whirlwind mother's place, but more and more I find me wistful, watchful of this new enormous impassivity. I stare for minutes at a time into her vacant face, daring the original to resurrect and rise.

I had the good sense not to call the aunt in residence at my mother's childhood home. If I have not been asked to visit once in fifty years, what are the chances that today is the convenient day.

The orange neon sign on the decorated metal door says NO SOLICITATIONS. I ring the doorbell anyway. Fool that I be. The aunt, who pulls aside the polyester curtain to peer out, points one arthritic finger in the general direction of the sign. I point my own gloved finger at my mother's head.

"What do you want?" She makes her voice large enough to penetrate the double doors.

"This is Alma. I'm Margaret." I all but scream.

"I know who you are." She opens one door part way. "What do you want?"

"Mother wanted to show me the house where she grew up."

Liar, liar, pants on fire, chants the Eileen in my head.

"I wanted to see it." I give honesty a try. "And to see you." (No need to go overboard on this truth thing.) "We wanted to see how you're doing."

"Well, not too well. This is a bad day."

No it's not, I want to yell back at her. It's a fine day. I had a lovely ride out here with my silent mother who, I think, seemed happy all the way. And I felt good. Resourceful, even. And not scared at all.

"Well, do you want to come inside? I can't stand here by the door all day."

I find this extremely small, old woman refreshing. She will require no niceties. We will not be obliged to drink her tea, or eat, or sit and be polite and speak of things we have no interest in.

"Mother just wanted to show me the house," I say.

"Well it's not a bit the same. We redid it, the whole thing. It was a pigsty before. Not a bit like this."

"Ummmm," I say, not taking any pains to cover my small shudder at the plastic clutter, bright orange afghans, thick shag carpet, lava lamps.

"Ummmm," I could swear I hear my mother echo; although I know she hasn't made a sound in months. She, who was a singer.

"Well, I have to go back to the bedroom now," the aunt says. "It's time for my treatment."

I imagine something wet and sticky, hot and moist, perhaps with Vaseline. And then I realize she is asking us to leave.

"Oh, you go right ahead," I say. "We'll just look around. Mother can show me her old bedroom."

"I can't let you go upstairs." She speaks as though the fire department made her promise.

"Well, you go do your treatment, and we'll sit right here."

I'm happier than I have been in years. I want to stay and be a thorn in this woman's side till Christmastime.

"Is she still the same?" The old woman indicates my mother with the quick jerk of her elbow.

My mother's studying her thumbprint.

"The same as what?" I say.

"You know," the old aunt says.

"Yes," I say. "She is the same. She's quite her old self in every way. It's just, she's silent, is the only thing."

And for the first time since the stroke, I wish she were her old self again. Her old self, who would be tearing up the carpet, maybe literally. Her old self, who would have walked in and said something in the neighborhood of, "Good grief, Woman," and while the old aunt was closing the front door, my mother would have taken down the kitchen curtains, sighed a good sigh, and said, "There, at least you've got a little light."

She might well have moved all the china figurines to one drum table top until it looked like a convention of porcelain shepherds, blown-glass ballerinas, china presidents. She would certainly have offered to cut and style the old aunt's hair, add maybe just a hint of henna. For a little life. And, she would have gone away in genuine bewilderment that the old aunt had found the wherewithal to take offense.

"Your mother likes to leave her mark," my father said. He was perhaps the only person she did not infuriate. But then, he only lived with her about a sixteenth of the time.

"Well, you sit here then if you're determined." The aunt is not a happy camper. "But my treatment isn't going to wait." I envision little gremlins wearing rubber gloves, who she knows will start without her.

"You go ahead," I say. "We'll be just fine."

My original mother would have led the way to the back bedroom, involved herself in every aspect, improvising and improving.

But as it is, the second the bedroom door clicks shut my mother hobbles out into the pantry, and with obvious concentration and some effort, opens up the cupboard door. Slowly, studiously, she starts taking out the canned goods, one at a time, using both her hands. I know I should try to stop her, but the way I'm feeling here today, I hope she turns out every item in the place, upends the bureau drawers, pours maple syrup on everything.

And then, just like that, it comes *back* to me. This was the aunt who tried to have the children—Eileen and my brothers and me—"removed." It was right after my little sister Annie died, before they knew it was TB. I'm almost certain I am remembering right. Hazel. The aunt's name returns with the memory. She came to our house, and yelled and screamed and tried to drag us out and put us in my uncle's truck.

I can't believe I brought my mother here today. I can't believe that Eileen let me. If it had been a matter of my showing up for dinner at the Country Club in knee socks, Eileen would have moved heaven and earth to stop me, but, presented with the news that I intended to walk my mother through the gates of fiery hell, Eileen offered nothing but her knee-jerk demur.

My mother's still removing cans and ketchup bottles. This woman has enough ketchup for another lifetime.

"Come on, Mother, we should go." I want to run screaming from this place. I touch my mother's skinny arm, which feels surprisingly strong and steady. The whole bottom shelf of the cupboard's empty now, and I watch as my mother reaches back and makes a little click that frees a foot-long section of the shelf. She tries to lift the board, but it's no use. She hasn't got the strength. She turns her eyes to me. For the first time in such a long, long while, she really looks at me. I reach across in front of her and with a few strong tugs, I lift the board away.

My mother grunts, as sure as day. She reaches down into the dark space and pulls out a rubber ball, and cloth, and two round sticks, all somehow attached together. She lifts it to her cheek and then I see, it's meant to be a doll. The ball is the head with black-inked mouth and nose and eyes, smudged inky hair; the larger stick is the body and the doll's one leg; the smaller stick, that is tied with wire to make a cross, is the two arms; the rotted cloth's a dress. My mother doesn't look at me, but quickly as she's able, she puts the doll back in the wooden well and motions for me to put the board in place. Then she pushes the cans of Carnation milk and Campbell's mushroom soup, the string beans and the tuna fish across the counter until all the tins are back inside, and then with her good shoulder, she closes up the cupboard door.

"I might have known you'd be snooping all around the place." The aunt's voice gives me a minor heart attack. I feel like I have just been caught red-handed in the Tower with the crown jewels stuffed inside my tee shirt. My mother doesn't flinch. She no longer can. But oh, one day she would have bristled, raised her purple plume and fired her cannons, two at a time.

"God hates a petty person above all other things," she would have said with something like soft sorrow in her tone. "Enlarge your thinking, Hazel. Let it *out* of this room. Take it for a walk. Buy it a kite. I could make you a kite, Hazel. I've never done it, but I've seen it done. Do you have such a thing as a long lightweight piece of balsam wood and maybe fifty or sixty feet of cotton twine? If you don't, the wooden slat from that window shade might do. Oh, and butcher's paper," she would say to this farm woman who for the whole of her only lifetime, single-handed, slaughtered every morsel of her own meat.

And we'd be off to the races. My mother in the throes of her desire for periwinkle paint for the butterflies she thinks should decorate the kite, Aunt Hazel apoplectic, in the end waving a broom and threatening to call the lunatic asylum, which went out of business before anybody in the room was born. But institutions linger longer than their business days. When I was growing up in the 1950s, the institute of terror, the oft-chanted dread, was the *county home,* a temporary residence for indigents during the Great Depression.

This younger and more lively version of Aunt Hazel would ultimately have had us running down the path, I like to think, ducking soft tomatoes she hurled willy-nilly from the basket on the porch.

"The Bible says *Be still and know that I am God*," my mother would have said as we scurried away. "And that's definitely the beaten track to Him, but I can tell you for a fact I am convinced that the Almighty God of all Creation is also a big fan of activity."

We're standing now outside Aunt Hazel's version of the house where my mother grew to be this thing that she would be. There has been no broom, no threat of kites, no overripe tomatoes hurled today. We were asked to leave. We went quietly. As I so often have. My mother stands here looking out across the fields where on another day she might have filled the sky with kites. But from now on, any kites are up to me.

I manipulate Mother into the car and only then does it hit me. We left the rubber ball doll there. I got so caught up in my mother's obvious fear of Aunt Hazel's discovering her hiding place, I didn't register that my mother was leaving it behind.

Does she in her bewilderment imagine that she will come back to check again that it is there, in fifty more years' time, or that she will reclaim it on the morning of the Final Judgment Day?

Or is it her intention in perplexity to show me where it is so I can come back and get it when I need to? Does she imagine God will grant me now long life, that twenty years from now I will come back, when some whole new family owns the place, connive to get myself invited in, under cover of some ruse, maybe returning as a religious, perhaps of my mother's kind, a blood relative of her God, whom I must say I prefer to the gods of anybody else I've met so far. Her God, so entirely splendid, so righteous, with no patience whatsoever with the religious shenanigans in my, or any other, neighborhood, reliable *and* unpredictable, interesting really, not pliant, definitely not that, nobody's fool, good company.

"You will give yourself up to Him one day," my mother used to say to me. "And He will burn you up, consume you like pile of dried brown leaves, and you will be a phoenix, do you know what that is?"

"How can I come to God? I'm such a sinner," I would say.

"Why that's exactly the sort of person God has an interest in dynamiting, dissolving with His mercy. Oh you'll love it. When it's time." She speaks as though I have been begging, and she's telling me I'll have to wait.

I try to think if this rubber ball doll might be tied up with God some way. I can't think how, but everything my mother did was part and parcel of that partnership.

So. I'm meant to come back one day to get it, while the new owner is getting a treatment by the gremlins in the bedroom in the back. Or, maybe Eileen will read in the paper that the old place burned to the ground, and she will, for once in her blighted life, think to mention something important when she calls me on the telephone, and I will drive all night to get there, stopping only once at 4 a.m. out on the loneliest stretch of highway in America, to get down on my knees beside the car to pray, and God will answer me, as a personal favor to my mother, his longtime friend, and I will arrive just as the dump truck comes to cart the stuff away. I will put on grubby garden gloves and the gum boots I find out in the barn, and I will stand knee-deep in rubble—still smoldering? No, I think just powdery and dry—and God will whisper *Over there, look over there, underneath that charred metal pot.* And there she'll be. This rubber-headed doll in half a dress, all sooty, but just fine, and still—after a hundred years of waste and reason—the only doll just like her that was ever made.

THE NEXT LIFE

THE GRAY-SKINNED COUPLE SMOKING CIGARETTES ask for two beers and two cups of tea. I give them what they want. It's my first night here. I got this job by saying I had been a waitress at a truck stop. If I had known how readily a lie can take the truth's place, I might have set up a new life years ago.

I couldn't say my truck stop was in a small town in Massachusetts where, in fact, the closest I came to anything so organized and purposeful was as a volunteer. I volunteered to be a wife—twice—to wash the socks and underwear and to keep track of dental appointments and social engagements and emotional life. Nobody made me. Nobody paid me. I volunteered. It gets old. Actually, what it gets is over.

"Two more beers, miss, if you please."

"With tea?" I'm smiling.

The wife frowns at me. She thinks I'm flirting with her husky husband.

"No, but you could bring a basket of them chips and salsa," he says.

The wife frowns again. She thinks he's flirting back with me.

I sashay over to the bar. I feel as though I have been a waitress all my life, and my mother and two aunts before me. I see myself in a tight, polyester, robin's egg blue uniform stretched out across my bed, counting tips, and chewing gum.

"So what time do they start pouring in?" I ask my new boss Joe.

"Who?" he says, like I just made an ethnic slur about his people.

I look beguiling and smile. I bet there's not a two-inch hair-free zone on Joe's whole body.

My first thought when our next live one walks through the door is: axe-murderer. Jake the Rake. It might be the haircut. The man is small and spare and mostly bald and stooped at the shoulders like someone who has been ducking his head his whole life—keeping a low profile—even though he can't be over five-foot-seven. This has to be what a mass murderer looks like when he is in a diner. The man's a study in nervous foibles. I don't think he's here to make new friends.

"Well." Joe saunters over to the man. "What'll it be, buddy?"

The man looks up, clearly puzzled. *What will what be?*

"Oh, uh, do you have coffee?"

"That it?" Joe makes a project of looking bored.

"And meat?" The man speaks the two words into his shirt pocket. "Do you have meat?"

"You mean like meatballs, or pork chops, or ham, or steak, or what?" It seems there is no meat Joe could not produce on demand. I'm hoping this man will ask for spring lamb with green mint jelly and small, butter-roasted new potatoes.

"Meatballs," he says.

I look out the window. Beyond the smudged plate glass is only empty dark—or maybe nothing, maybe the world ends at the windowpane. That's what kind of night it is.

Two teenagers walk in. A couple. Do they still call two people that? They look like they have been together for a hundred years, like they drag their relationship around behind them everywhere. They're wearing the same faded denim on the same slumped frames. They probably have settled down to one position to make love in, have picked out one certain word they always call it.

They order double home fries and two beers. I know they're underage, but I'm hardly in any position to start judging other people. Besides, I'm glad they're here. I figure the boyfriend is big enough to deal with our diminutive axe-murderer should he have one of his episodes.

I deliver the beers with what I hope is a jaded eye. If they order seconds, I'll ask to see IDs. I want this young man sober enough to deal with any antics Jake the Rake gets up to; although, so far all he's done is push his meatballs around the plate and soak up all the sauce with bread. If he intends to do us harm here, it's going to take all night.

Three chubby ladies waddle in and squeeze their pleased and perfumed selves into a booth and ask if there is any pie. They've just been somewhere or they're on their way. They're all excited. You can just tell they were the kind of teenagers who inhaled bags of potato chips and pints of onion dip when they babysat, who told each other complicated lies and married at the age of twenty-nine, feeling lucky in eleven different ways.

I've started doing this lately: I see people the way they must have been at the age of five or ten or fifteen. Or sometimes I see what sort of crinkled-up or frog-fat old lady a person is slated to become in fifty years. The thing's so easy once you start, you wonder everybody doesn't go around doing it all day. Maybe they do.

I wish these women hadn't come. They water it all down, dilute the whole experience. Even Jake the Rake seems only puny, nervy, now they're here. It always happens. New people wander in and they dilute and redefine the people that you had all fixed in your mind a certain way. Like if a group of abusive husbands or a busload of high church clergy came through the door, I'd start to see these old girls in a whole new way. So much of life is by comparison. What's that old vaudeville joke? *How's your wife? Compared to what?*

How's your wife?

"You could never make it on your own," rubbed raw, and frightened and bereft himself, my husband shouted at the door. "You can't even earn a living."

As though I had not earned the very right to live, all these years, paid hard cash for the privilege, every blessed day.

"You'll never make it. You've been clinging to other people your whole life. You've been a tag-along for years. You won't have clue how to make a life for only you."

"Do you think I should get that plain or à la mode?" the youngest woman says.

These three heavily fleeced females invite me to feel tastefully superior or at least grateful that however much my whole life's a flagrant failure, at least I am not them. Like I said, comparison. When I put the pie down, I brush one fleece sleeve and get a shock. The fabric is soft and would feel so innocent to blind fingers; the women themselves are probably soft if you could keep them quiet for five minutes while the blind man groped them. But they are practicing, card-carrying deceivers; the very clothes they wear can make the sparks fly, they've dressed themselves in chemicals from head to toe and sprayed their soft, white, any-day-now flabby bodies with five or six different scented potions, releasing in the process enough ozone-eaters to create two new, small holes to welcome in the ultraviolet. Their lives flirt everyday with science fiction.

I walk over to support the kitchen wall. What have I got against these silly women? They've done nothing wrong. Or they've done everything wrong, but what's that got to do with me. I'm in charge of pie distribution here. I am so always and eternally overreaching. I get so wrapped up with everyone I see: imagining them as schoolchildren and potty, dotty old women and old men, offering the benefit of my harsh judgment and my unerring eye. Someone should tell me: *Get a life*. It always sounds so harsh. It always sounds so right.

The door pushes open and a small, wizened woman walks in, blinking, tentative, taking time to accommodate the light. A small child, a little girl in a green woolen dress-up coat with a black velvet collar steps out from behind her.

The child glows. My first notion is that had we been paying closer attention we all would have seen the rays of yellow light spiking out in all directions from behind the old woman. Then it hits me. This child is not some supernatural light source. She's on fire. She's got a fever. Her eyes have that hot, blazing gaze, that black-eyed stare.

I meet them in the center of the tables.

"She's got a temperature," the old woman says. "She started with it on the bus. We were on our way to Cleveland. My sister buries her husband in the morning. Ten a.m.," she says. "Sharp."

I have the feeling there is some conventional response this news means to evoke, but I can't figure what it is. I am aware that the restaurant's gone silent around us. No one speaks. The last song on the jukebox fades with two final, half-hearted croons. I turn around. Everyone is watching. Even Jake the Rake is staring at the child across his empty plate. I feel like I'm in some play. I used to have a shrink who said I felt that way on purpose so I could keep myself from getting close to other people. I stick my tongue out at him. The old woman winces.

"Oh no," I say. "I wasn't…. That wasn't…."

She looks so old and tired.

"I came in here to get this girl a drink and aspirin tablets."

"Oh no, not aspirin," I say. "Aspirin can cause Reyes Syndrome in children under eighteen. Tylenol or Advil till they leave for college." (I've always figured God made it safe for kids to switch to aspirin at eighteen, because that's when they leave home and there isn't going to be anybody in the dorm or the barracks or the big city to make sure the place is aspirin free.) I know pretty much everything that could kill anyone, in what manner, and approximately how much time it would likely take.

"Could we get her a drink do you suppose?" the old woman says.

"Oh yes. Sorry. Of course. Here. Let her sit down. I'll get a Coke, no ice. I'll stir the bubbles out. Do you like Coke?" I ask the little girl.

She nods. "With bubbles." Her voice is husky. She sounds like a smoker, about forty-five.

Behind the counter, I pour the soda back and forth between two glasses to de-fizz the carbonation. I read one time that a person's stomach can't deal with all the bubbles and so it spews them up into the tiny, crowded Eustachian tubes where they can cause an infection. "I'd like to see the article that said that." My husband's voice snide even in memory.

The little girl inhales the Coke and I bring her a dish of ice to suck on, tiny cubes and melting slivers. One of the fat pie ladies gives me two children's Tylenol I get the little girl to crunch.

"I don't know what to do," the old woman says. "I wonder if we ought to find her a doctor or go someplace to sleep."

And in five minutes' time six of us are packed into the teenager's big boat of a Chevrolet. I volunteered to go along to the emergency room and the boy said he'd give us a lift and surprise, surprise, Jake the Rake said, "I might as well come too."

The grandmother's holding Annie on her lap in the front seat. I considered making a crusade to get the woman to put Annie in a separate seatbelt, but I've already kept her from getting Reyes Syndrome and an ugly Eustachian tube carbonation infestation. A person can only be obnoxious so many times in one evening. I've spent my whole lifetime keeping other people—starting with my mom and dad—from getting things they didn't know existed. It's time to quit.

I'm scrunched in back in the middle between the girl-friend—whose hair smells like thyme and lavender when it brushes up against me and whose whole face smells like Juicy Fruit gum—and this man whom I expect to murder all of us before we reach the hospital. He smells like metal. I think about saying something offhand about how I always carry a small automatic pistol. I think about asking him if he can pinpoint just when his life started to get out of hand.

The emergency room takes approximately forever. Jake the Rake decides as long as he's here he might as well have them take a look at a cut he's got that's turned all pussy. He peels off a dirty bandage and shows me the wound before I can look away. I knew I'd suffer at his hand tonight. Then the teenage girl remembers that her throat is sore. Her boy-friend tells her to get over it. I'm with him. It's all marketing. You find yourself in a jewelry store and suddenly you think you need a crystal bud vase. You're in an E.R. late at night and your whole body wants a pill, your limbs cry out for plaster casts and penicillin or, at the very least, professional attention.

What's the symptom I've brought here tonight? Let's see. Somebody shot my life. I shot it myself. I was in a two-person collision. My life just got run over with a tractor-trailer truck.

"The doctor says old Annie here will be just fine." The old women walks towards us. "Ear infection. He gave her pills. Her fever's down already from the aspirin."

Tylenol.

"The doctor thinks she shouldn't travel more tonight and the next bus leaves at midnight and how am I to make the funeral if we sleep here?"

"Where are her parents?" I think the night allows the question.

"Dead. She's an orphan girl."

I wince again. I realize this is likely not new information to the little girl, but it still seems harshly put.

"If I had a place for her to stay…." The old woman scans the waiting room.

"She could stay with me," I hear myself say. "I'm staying in a house with extra bedrooms. My landlady's a nurse."

"Well, if you're sure." The old lady's bumping off to Cleveland in her mind.

I'm disappointed. I want to keep the child tonight, I might like to keep her forever, but I want this grandmother to ask for character witnesses and proof of citizenship and a certificate that says that I've had all my shots.

"I'll pick her up in two days. I'll call you if it's any longer."

I want to shake this woman. I want to tell her I could be a white slaver or a drug addict or a lunatic. For the first time, I look down at the little girl. Annie. The sight of that small face snaps me back to sane behavior. She's five years old. That's a full-time job for starters. Plus, it's past her bedtime, and she's in a strange place with a fever and an earache and her parents are dead.

An hour later she's asleep, tucked up in my bed. I couldn't have her wake up alone in a strange house. The teenagers are probably making out on the sprung-spring sofa in her parents' den and Jake the Rake is off to Cleveland with Annie's granny. When we dropped her off at the bus terminal, Jake hopped out mumbling something about how he might as well go too. I say good riddance. I know he won't hurt the grandmother. Her mind's on other things. Joe probably closed shop early and went home to bed. The three fat ladies, no doubt adenoidal, are now snoring in three different beds.

I squirm around and try to nestle down in the big dead chair. It's like some wild beast somebody shot and dragged home to use as furniture. Then I remember: the old couple at the restaurant with beer and tea, my first customers of my whole one-night waitressing career. I can't believe I just forgot them, whited them from memory in an hour's time. That's how it goes. No matter how many people you cart off to the emergency room in the middle of the night or invent imaginary destinations and life stories for, there's always someone gets left out. Overlooked, like the tea-beer couple, or left behind on purpose, like Joe, the old cook and bottle-washer. Like David, the old husband.

David the old husband who would surely have a speech to make if he were here tonight. "You think you can just keep this little girl," he would say. "You think you can just take her home and buy her clothes and be her mother. *You.*"

"Oh, shut up," I say out loud.

Annie doesn't stir.

"I have a clue for you." The onetime husband yells across four states. "You can't make up a life going through the world collecting people who need watching over and a place to sleep and somebody to sit up all night beside the bed."

Annie blinks awake, as though responding to the harshness of the words inside my head.

"Where'd Granny go?"

"Remember? She went on the bus, and she'll be back to pick you up before you know it."

The child frowns.

"Do you always sleep in that chair?" she asks me.

"Oh no, I don't even really live here. I live far away."

"Are you waiting for your granny or somebody to come pick you up?"

"I never even knew my granny, either one. They both died before I was born."

"My parents died before I was born."

I forbear to speak to the unlikelihood of this timing. We each of us have our own stories that we tell.

"Are you sleepy?"

"Nope," I say.

"Me neither. I'm never sleepy. I could stay up for a hundred nights."

"Me too." Actually, it feels like I have.

"I have ten ponies. They're my own."

"That's amazing."

"My granny isn't coming back. She was taking me to Cleveland to leave me in an orphanage."

With her ten ponies.

Actually, the child's story sounds a bit believable.

"No, sweetheart," I say. "Your granny went to her sister's house."

"She hasn't got a sister. It's just her and me and no more family and now she's old, she says she wants me settled."

I know she's telling stories, as we used to say, but at the same time I'm filling out adoption applications in my mind.

"Is everything all right here?" My landlady, the nurse, taps on the door as she pushes it open. I may need to reconsider the idea of living here forever. I'm pretty fond of locks and privacy. "Are you girls all right?"

"Fine," I say. "We're just talking. We're not sleepy."

"I never get sleepy," Annie says.

"Me neither," says the nurse.

And does *she* have ten ponies too?

"This was my room when I was a little girl," the nurse says. "I made those tiny notches on the windowsill with my front teeth. I still remember the neat feeling, the soft crunches of the paint."

"You know, of course," I say to Annie, "not to do that yourself. There's lead in the paint, and it's not good for you."

I catch the nurse's scowl. "It used to be okay," I say, to placate. Actually, it used to be lethal, but all kids did it. I think my own palate remembers paint. My teeth imprints are probably everywhere. We all grew up doing these horrendously dangerous things in our pre-seatbelt childhoods. The whole thing's an illusion anyway. People pretend they can protect a child from harm, and if all goes perfectly the child grows up and falls victim to adulthood anyway.

"Ever thought of a relationship where you are not the den mother in charge of safety on the planet. Maybe a relationship where you are not in charge at all," my husband's mean voice hectors.

"PHHHHTTTT," I snort at him.

"What's that you say?" the nurse asks me.

"PHHHHTTTT." Old Annie imitates my noise.

If we were all blood relatives, now someone would have to say, "Well, don't you think it's time you tried to get some sleep."

As it is, we three might talk all night.

"My little brothers were born in that room." The nurse taps the wall. "Nobody had babies at home then, but my mother was a pistol. She had twins when she was only expecting one baby. She nicknamed the second baby Extra for a joke and that's what we still call him, well, X. The first twin, John, died in the war. My brother X is a pilot."

"And your mom was a pistol," Annie says. "My mom was a ballerina and a movie star."

I'm guessing if your mom dies before you're born, she can have been anything.

"She was going to be very famous," Annie said.

"I was going to be famous," the nurse says. "I was going to be Clara Barton and Florence Nightingale."

"Aren't you still?"

"Oh, no. I got too old."

"And that's your reason?" Annie's starting to look tired.

"It'll do."

"What were you going to be?" Annie turns to me.

"You know, for years I've been telling people I wanted to work in a diner, like the one you came into tonight."

"See." Annie eyelids droop, heavy. "See," she tells the nurse. "You can be anything you want. A movie star or Clara Barton or a famous waitress. My granny's going to be a jewel in the crown of Jesus. You just have to pick one thing." And Annie's eyelids close and she's asleep. She's riding on a pony all the way to Cleveland where she'll live in a swanky orphanage forever until her grandmother comes back on Tuesday to pick her up.

"Do you believe that stuff she said?" The nurse scrunches her lips up tight. "Do you?"

"No," I say. "Well, maybe."

"Kids don't have a clue. When I slept in that bed, there was nothing in the world I wasn't going to do. Then time came along and took my life and shook it down to hardly anything at all, and I grew up and moved across the hall. I wonder if anybody's life is what they wanted."

"Probably astronauts," I say. "And firemen."

And she who never tires grows sleepy says a quick goodnight and leaves the night to only me.

When I was in the seventh grade, a girl named Shawneen VanTassel used to threaten me in the parking lot beside the school, the first thing in the morning. "I'm gonna kill you and your dopey friend with the ponytail, and if you tell anyone then I'll really do it." I went to school each day prepared to die and prayed prayers swift and to the purpose every time I left the school to go back home again.

Shawneen VanTassel was listed on the front page of the directory of my high school class for my twenty-fifth reunion, the page of graduation photographs of the classmates who were dead.

She had lived only six years after high school graduation.

I pull the scratchy wool blanket up around my shoulders. It smells like 1960.

So what's the story? What's old Shawneen VanTassel come to preach tonight? Just this, I think: She's here to tell the snoring nurse and me, whatever you are set on course to do, jump in with both feet, go face first. If you're bent on besting old Florence Nightingale at her own game or starting your own orphanage or being a jewel in the crown of Jesus or threatening the health and safety of two puny, pimpled seventh graders in the parking lot before school in the morning, then do it with a vengeance, scare the pants off those two girls, leave teeth marks in their memory of seventh grade so deep that just the mention of your name gives pause a full thirty years after you are dead and gone.

I turn out the light and add my own P.S.: Nobody, not one of us, knows what's going to happen, and it is bright purple, patent arrogance to give up hope because you think you're so damn smart you know your life is sure to be a sinkhole from now on. Despair is arrogant and pompous and God might well think it's rude.

Annie stirs, and I reach out in the darkness one more time and touch that smooth, warm cheek.

She feels cooler. She'll sleep now through the night. I might, myself.

MY COUNTRY 'TIS OF THEE

I'M NOT REALLY ALL THAT COMFORTABLE with foreign people. I always catch myself being overly friendly, nicer than I really am, my nouns and verbs more carefully selected: doggedly enunciated, punctuated with tight smiles. And volume is a problem. I start out pretty loud and after fifteen minutes, I hear myself yelling. Words far too kind, in a fortissimo that wears everybody out.

Plus I am always asking foreigners how much things cost, and how far a certain city is, and who's related to whom and how, and do they feel uncomfortable in America. I call it that. "America," I say, when what I mean is the U.S.

My young Cambodian friend, Boren, is at my house tonight with his young Chinese wife. We're eating in the kitchen. I ran into Boren at Wal-Mart where he works, where I buy everything I buy—which isn't all that much— even though I know in stultifying detail the five most compelling reasons why you're supposed to spit at Wal-Mart when you drive by on your way to the overpriced, pretentious stores on Main Street, where, incidentally, everything is made by the same exploited, knurled and calloused child-sized hands in the selfsame village in Romania.

That's the problem. If you know anything at all, you cannot do a blessed thing without committing some vile injustice. Everything's as evil as everything else, so the bottom line is: knowledge, even vague awareness, can hog-tie you.

I felt guilty when I ran into Boren. I was buying this soy milk that has sixty calories and nine grams of protein in a glass. No animals were killed in its procurement. A purchase devoid of any sin, or any that I knew of. But nonetheless, I felt greedily consumptive, with four liters in my basket. Foreigners always make me feel so American, a card-carrying member of the U.S. club.

And club membership is a tricky thing for me. I hardly ever fit.

"You thrive on ostracism," my sister told me once. I beamed.

"It's not a compliment," she said.

But I do try to not be part of any group I'm in. It's not that hard. People are usually pretty happy to exclude me.

"When are you free?" I said to Boren, moving my scarf to cover a couple bottles of the high-priced soy. "I'd love to meet your wife. I'd love to have you come for dinner."

"I only on Saturday night do not work then," he said and smiled the way he always smiled when asked to prune the Rose of Sharon closer to the trunk, or make perhaps finer distinctions between the weeds and asters in my flower bed, back when he helped me with the garden.

"So come to dinner tomorrow night." I spoke without thinking, guilt-propelled. A large measure of what I do each day is fueled by one brand of guilt or another. Without it, I probably would get very little done.

"Yes, to come there we would be happy," Boren said to me, quite clearly oblivious of anything my shopping basket might contain.

"Do you eat meat?" I said. "Does your wife eat meat?"

Boren beamed. "Yes, meat. Yes."

So much for Buddha.

I almost never invite people for a meal. I can't cook.

Well, that's one of the reasons.

During the day I called about twenty-five different people and said *I would so love to have you meet my young friend from Cambodia. He spent eleven years in a refugee camp in Thailand after the Khmer Rouge wiped out his family. He walked for thirteen weeks to get there. Last year he went back to Thailand and met and married the sweetest wife.* I figured one of the twenty-five might respond to the guilt spur same as me, but no takers.

Even if people are free, they don't like the short notice. I understand. I mean, we need time to get used to the idea that we'll be going to eat and talk and drink in someone else's house. You can't get used to an idea that like in one day. Plus, last minute means that you're an afterthought. It's very complicated. That's another reason I don't entertain.

Also, there's the part about nobody ever asking me. Though that makes sense. I'm single. I am a walking odd number. I was *even* for a while, and then I hired a lawyer and I went to court and they made me odd again.

I worried I'd have nothing to say to Boren and his new wife, Ling, that I would batter them with questions—loud, carefully pronounced, personal questions—driving them and me insane. I do have a history.

But the meal is nice. They eat and eat and eat. Something of a novelty in my experience. The wife is very good at silence, and I watch and think perhaps it is a thing that I might learn tonight, but not before I have exhausted them and me and all things living with every question I can think of.

Boren was carrying a flat plastic bag when he came in. So much more intriguing than a wine bottle, I think. If I ever get invited over to anybody's house again, I intend to devote all the notice I am given to coming up with something gift-wrapped and astonishing to bring along.

"So, what's in the bag?" I finally ask the newlyweds. It's that or "How old was you grandmother when her periods started?" I think I've pretty much covered everything else.

"This is the photographs of our wedding, you know," Boren says.

I take the proffered album. I'm fast approaching the age when I will be too old to look at wedding pictures. I can't remember what it is that you're supposed to see.

Ten minutes later I look up from the pages.

"What is this?" I say.

"This is the photographs of our wedding, you know."

"Boren, Ling, these pictures are amazing."

I turn my eyes back to the pages. Photos of the couple, and of the bride alone, image after image of a porcelain-skinned face, features delicate and lovely, an advertisement for grace, a snapshot of what God must have had in mind when he created Eve.

"I don't understand," I say. "In every photo there's a different dress."

"Costume." Boren enunciates as if the word were in Khmer. "All day from six in the morning until the afternoon we change and change to a new costume."

I look again. In some the bride's black hair flows free, in some she wears it coifed into a sixties beehive, in others it hugs her scalp in deep-oiled sheen.

I look from the perfect bride to the young woman who has just eaten two pork chops and seven miniature helpings of canned corn. The acne on her face screams adolescence, her tiny teeth are tinted brown, her glasses ride low on her little nose. Her face is sweet. It is a face you would be happy to see every day for any number of decades in a row. The face in the photograph is not a person. People are not beautiful that way, not in real life.

I don't even like photographs. I never look at them in magazines. I like things that are made up. But these. I cannot get enough of them. I could look at them all night.

"Where did you get these costumes?"

"We rent them, you know."

"But they are so rich. How much must that cost to do?"

"About one hundred or two hundred dollar, I think," Boren says.

"Look," I say, "everyone in the world needs to see these pictures. We need to sell them to a magazine. Would you like that?" I turn to Ling. "Would your family, your parents, in Cambodia, would they mind?"

"They would I think be very happy." Ling speaks her first full sentence of the evening.

We spend the next hour scanning the photos onto my computer. Boren and Ling stand behind me, polite, patient. They question nothing that I do. It's that way with refugees. Everything we do is probably about as strange as everything else we do. Our actions so bizarre that nothing can be aberrant.

If this were some regular dinner party, people would be drinking coffee, and talking about where they went on their vacation, and what they ate when they were there, and how it tasted, and just what they hope to eat and see and do when they next go away from here.

Boren and Ling are only where they are. I do not think they believe— or that they disbelieve—that I will sell these photographs to *Harper's Bazaar* or *Modern Bride* for four thousand dollars, so they can buy a car and sleep an extra hour on the February mornings they now spend standing at bus stops on their way to one of the five jobs they work between them.

I went to the town office yesterday to pay a parking ticket, and a woman there was telling everyone that she was driving south on Route 89 in her suburban Volvo, and a tractor-trailer truck she was passing veered straight over into her lane, and going seventy miles an hour, she slammed on the brakes and steered her car onto the median, where for the past eleven weeks God has been piling up the snow that stopped her car. The driver of the tractor-trailer truck saw her veer, slammed on his brakes, and skidded across the median, across the for-that-instant-empty lane of oncoming traffic and down the slight embankment on the other side. They both got out and walked away.

All she could say, over and again, was: *I am alive, I am alive…. The trucker is alive and I'm alive.*

Boren's family, four generations—parents, children, cousins, aunts, and uncles—were massacred. Not one of them died before he suffered torture, and Boren crawled for thirteen weeks through dense jungles till he reached Thailand, where he waited, not impatiently, for eleven years before he was allowed to come to the U.S. Ling's family escaped with their lives from China to Thailand, and she met Boren there. Boren applied and was rejected, four years in a row, to bring Ling back here as his wife.

And here they stand tonight, in my computer room, and watch me scan the only copies of the pictures of their wedding in Cambodia, and they do not, have not, nor will they ever, speak the words: *I am alive.*

And the lady with the Volvo which she drove away in, stands in crowds of strangers in city offices saying, over and again: *The trucker is alive, I am alive,* and everybody shakes their heads and says: *Can you believe it.*

I'm telling you about America.

MOTHER'S HELPER

YOU TRAVELED ON A DIRT ROAD, across the railroad tracks, then down a tiny dip the road took through a patch of swampy woods to reach the two tarpaper-shingled houses. First, the Deans' house, then Erma's. The Deans were Erma's relatives—I want to say Mrs. Deans was Erma's sister—a scatty woman with a skinny husband and any number of puny, pale-lashed children, living in their black shack of a house no more than ten yards from Erma's door.

I have set half the British novels I have read inside the Deans' house. Dickens and Thackery and Charlotte Bronte have all had poverty-clothed families living there: characters who lived and died, and did not spend one night of their brief, blighted, if well-written, lives anywhere but in that house.

But it is not the Deans' house I go back to now. It is to Erma's house, next door. A house where no fiction ever happened. There was barely enough room for the real life transpiring there.

"Now I hope you kids don't devil me to death today." This would be my mother, dressed up in her church clothes, riding in the front seat of a 1950, strange maroon boat of a Buick, driving out to Erma's house for Sunday dinner. "You give me some peace this afternoon, or you'll live to regret it, I can promise you that."

No one in the back seat required her guarantee. In fact, we took her words as some assurance of a different sort. We knew it for the bluster that it was. My mother never threatened and then hit us. It was always either/or. Plus, she only hit us when we were at home. It helped define the place. We could not have told the reason for either aspect. We didn't know why she hit us in the first place—beatings, rash and random, born of a fury we could neither comprehend nor forecast—but we knew we were safe at Erma's house.

Erma was my mother's friend, her best, as far as I could tell, her only friend. She was a kind woman, trusting, easily deceived and taken in.

We went to Erma's house a lot, Sunday dinners mostly, or Saturday night suppers, when I would, at some point, fall asleep across Erma's coat-covered bed in the room just off the noisy kitchen, to be carried fast asleep out to the cold car, to be propped up between my sleeping brothers, sleeping sister. I see my father lift us, one sleep-warm, saggy body at a time, four trips back and forth again, to lean all of us together like so many old sacks of potatoes. My father, not my mother, would have carried us. I was long-limbed and floppy, as gangly sleeping as awake, and just as unlikely for my mother to lay hold of in any neutral way.

I liked the sleeping part, and the food: the soft, warm ham; the mashed potatoes with yellow butter; thick, smooth, salty gravy; tiny, skittish peas; red jello salad with walnuts and banana slices and pineapple. First, there was too much of everything, and then there was the pie. Coconut custard, lemon meringue, banana cream, with sweet whipped filling two full inches high, and white fluff twice as high on top of that. No one makes pies like that anymore. No one made pies like that back then.

And I liked Bill, Erma's husband—Billy boy—who slipped us sticks of chewing gum in church, when he led us to our seats. Ushers ushered then. None of this seat-yourself in those churchgoing days. You pointed in the general direction of your preference and the usher undertook to lead you there, like they sometimes do at weddings and at funerals today. I liked Bill because he could joke with you without asking the stupid questions other ushers asked the eight-year-olds, like "Are you married yet?"

I liked Bill, and the food and sleep. The tricky part came in between. I was expected to play with Spike and Jessie, Erma and Bill's daughters, whose real names were Sandra and Jesmynd. By the time that I was eight or nine, they were teenagers, with breasts and boyfriends, and they read *Romance Magazine* and wore red lipstick and complicated, white brassieres. On Sunday afternoons I was expected to want to walk with them all the way into Bakerville to get ice cream, *that* after I had just eaten more in one meal than I ate in a week at home.

Wild boys in cars—hoodlums, I called them in my head—with packs of cigarettes rolled in their white T-shirt sleeves, and hair in grease-slicked ducktails, stopped their cars beside us, eyeing Spike and Jessie and my ice cream, and saying things like, "Could I have a lick?" Remarks I only understood enough to worry me.

There was sex in the air, but it only came to me as danger. I imagined their intentions to be murderous, not amorous. Danger figured largely in my imagination then—it does today, always there in possibility: destruction, harm, poised to strike at any moment, kept at bay by swift, smart prayers and my long-practiced caution.

One Sunday, Jessie was off somewhere, and I was left with Spike to occupy the slow part of the afternoon, that interval when sticky minutes drag their feet, and the hours they comprise are logy, dopey, but still far too restless to fall asleep. Spike let me play *servant* for a while. She lay on the bed, glamorous and languid in her white slip and tight cotton brassiere, the line between her breasts a deep slit I could imagine sliding slim slivers into. Dimes maybe, or thin buttons.

It was ninety degrees, and all the heat downstairs had been sent up the rail-less stairs behind us, to be shut up in that small room with its rough wood walls and ceiling and its hot, worn linoleum floors, now strewn with Spike's red blouse, blue skirt, nylons, garter belt.

I had played *servant* with these sisters now for years, but over time they had grown weary of the aimless game, wanting instead to read *True Love* and *Real Romance*, and listen to the radio.

I live in Massachusetts now, five hundred miles and forty years away from Spike and Buddy Holly and that stifling heat. My friend Ginny Carlson, who lives two doors over is a psychotherapist, a PhD, with a license and a tasteful office with a separate entrance and a steady stream of paying customers, and she would have me believe that any memory that reeks of sex and Sunday afternoon confusion was sex indeed and child abuse for sure. She thinks if something sounds erotic—in retrospect to a psychotherapist who was off in Minnesota negotiating a childhood of her own when the event in question happened—then it was most certainly erotic, and probably traumatic, and should now be resurrected and talked about, ideally twice a week.

She's wrong. I listen to her hundred-dollar theories, eat her German bakery strudel, drink her iced herb tea, and nod my head and know for certain deep inside of me she gets it wrong a full half the time. Crapshoot odds. Fifty-fifty. Close your eyes and theorize. You can go back and second-guess what happened on a hundred different Sunday afternoons and get it wrong as often as you get it right.

I know Spike did not abuse me that day, or let anybody else abuse me either. She did not entice me from that room, with promises of wild surprise, with any ill intent. We did not crawl out her bedroom window onto the hot tar roof that would have branded any flesh it touched. Or if we did, if we slip-slid down the shallow slope and made the easy drop into the waist-high grass below, and if we ran till we were out of breath and out of sight of Erma's house and hurried sweaty down the road to an old barn, as hot inside as a blast furnace, as scratchy on your skin as if you had thrown yourself into the straw and rolled all over like a crazy person, and if we met a boy there, a man really, and if he scowled at me, and Spike did say, "Hi, how ya' doin'? This is Alma's girl. She won't say nothin'," and then climbed up the steep ladder with him close behind, once turning, leering back at me, and if I did stand frozen, taking chills like when a fever's high enough to worry everybody in the room, and if they made a lot of noise, so that I knew for certain he was killing Spike up there and would surely come back down any moment to kill me, well—whatever you might pay Ginny Carlson, PhD, to say—they neither one of them did any harm to me.

And if I do not remember how I left that place, what power or volition carried me outside that barn and got me down the dusty road again, and up the ladder to the fire-blazed roof, and back inside that oven room where safety and perplexity had become one and the same thing, well, that is not to say that anything of any moment happened to me in that barn. I will only say that I was young and impressionable and perhaps not difficult to frighten, and that I remember— or forget—selectively, just as now in middle age I startle easily if someone comes up behind me in the kitchen when I am washing lettuce at the sink.

Besides, it is not the seldom Sunday afternoons of young, taut terror and confusion that leave scars. No, it is, I think, in daily life where harm is visited upon the young. It isn't heat or fright or flash incomprehension, noises in hot barns, the screaming overhead. It is the slow drip day-to-day that makes the marks and wears the soul away. I have told Ginny Carlson this a hundred times. I brought, I think, my own fright with me to that barn, just as I travel around with it today. Spike brought just herself and one of the long hours that she had to pass through to reach suppertime.

I crawled back in through the window to play out the remainder of that afternoon that wasn't finished with me, not quite yet. Later on, when Spike came back, she whispered a word I'd never heard before, and asked me if I knew what that word meant. I said *of course.* I made a point of knowing everything Spike knew. She had been kept back in school twice, for pity sakes.

"You're not going to snitch on me, are you?" Spike said. She lay there on the bed all frowsy and rumpled looking, pulling out curly cotton nubs one at a time from the old chenille bedspread. More than half the rows were down to pinhole dots. She was collecting the wrinkled threads and rolling them into a ball, intent and offhand all at once. "You're not going to tell, are you?"

I didn't answer, sensing that my silence gave me the upper hand some way, even though I thought it should be obvious, even to Spike, that I could live two lifetimes and never find the words to tell what happened in that barn. Speaking of it would be worse than living through it. I knew I'd never tell a soul. I never have.

"You promise me you'll never tell, and I'll tell you a secret," Spike said.

I tried to imagine a secret of hers that could interest me.

"Your mum might get arrested," Spike said. "She beats you kids, doesn't she?" She was accusing me of something. "I heard my mum tell my dad."

"Of course she doesn't," I said. "Don't be stupid. And how come people call you Spike, anyway? Your name is Sandra. Why don't you use your name? Spike is a boy's name."

"I don't know. My dad's always called me Spike. Anyway, I'm just telling you. Don't let her hit you anymore. My mum says it's a sin, plus she could get arrested. It's against the law."

"It is not."

"It is too. She could get sent to jail if she beats you up, even one more time. Don't let her do it. I wouldn't let somebody beat me up."

"Yeah, like you didn't let that man try to kill you in the barn. You are so stupid. My mother never even beat me once. You are the dumbest girl I ever knew."

I don't remember playing with Spike and Jessie again after that day, though I might have. I probably did. I probably had to walk with them to get an ice cream; I probably listened to their radio; I probably watched them read their magazines.

Then, sometime after that—those years do not exist in real time, so it might have been that fall, just after all the leaves and sun had gone away; or later, after early snows had fallen two days in a row; or, it might have been full calendar years later—Spike was gone away. Nobody spoke of her in anything but earnest whispers: *Won't marry her. In a home. Donald, after the father. No good. No earthly good.*

Then, all of a sudden, Jessie was married and off with her new husband in the army, in Mexico or Texas. Erma and my mother treated Jessie like a foreign missionary or the preacher's wife when she came back home for a visit. The three women sat in the back living room on straight-backed chairs, and my mother asked Jessie serious questions, and Erma shook her head at each reply.

"They sell them right out on the street there," Jessie said. My mother tsk-tsked. "You see them everywhere. It's not even hidden."

Erma and my mother made one, joint sigh, alive with disapproval and a saintly fascination. I spent weeks trying to work out what might be sold that could be this fully scandalous. I figured it had something to do with having babies, but I could not conjure up the product or merchandise. I am not sure I know today.

It occurs to me to wonder now where were the men, while all this life and conversation were transpiring—the women and their talk of sex and all things female filling up the kitchen and the living room, the men, the boys, nowhere in the picture.

Then, the next thing we knew, Erma had a sudden son. Spike's little boy, Donny. Erma raised him, gave him everything, and he grew up and joined the Merchant Marines. *Hardly ever comes to visit. Never even writes. After all Erma did for him*, all the ladies said. *And her a widow.* But, everybody always acts like their example of ingratitude would take first prize at the county fair.

My own mother always said, whenever Erma's life of sacrifice was being talked about, "Don't you think you'll have kids and come looking to me to care for them." She need not have worried.

Spike I saw one other time, years later. She was all dressed up, with a painted face and bad teeth and a kindness you could feel across the room. She was glad to see me. I was glad to see her. I don't remember what we said. Probably the usual. Nothing about sex or beatings, nothing about bastards and abuse, I am quite sure. I have the idea that Spike married and had a few more children. My mother may have told me this, or I might have made it up.

So, where's the story then? We went to eat at Erma's house, I played with her two daughters until they grew up, a little early perhaps, but all the same, they would have had to grow up sometime.

And now, a lifetime later, I call back that one summer day, a Sunday of immoderate temperature and sure discomfort; I recall it and declare: My mother never beat me up, not one time, after that stifling afternoon. Because, I knew from that day forward that the only way to keep her from being sent to jail was to make dead certain that she never once hurt us again, and the only way I knew to do that was to take off like a crazy person whenever she came at me, run out the door and down the street, no matter if it was the dead of winter in the middle of the night. I could have run a hundred miles without once stopping to catch my breath if it meant that I could keep my mother there with me. I was a strong girl. I could do anything. In fact, I did. The sudden swats went on forever, times she caught me unaware, but nothing anyone could go to jail for. My mother's rage was sudden and short-lived. I could always wait her out away.

I wish I could have told Spike thank you when I saw her that one time, but she would have only smiled and frowned at me, just as oblivious as she was on that hot Sunday, after the action and the talking was all done, and she lay back and closed her eyes and in two minutes' time was snoring like a pig.

I told my brothers and my sister that our mother could be put in prison for beating us and so to be on guard and always run away. I don't know if they did or not. You can't remember anybody else's childhood, sometimes not that much of your own. Incidents and years go missing. And I can't ask my sister now. We don't have the sort of conversation a question like that could be worked into. And my brothers are not men you'd ply with queries about their own or anybody's history. Ginny Carlson would have three different things to say about their electronic network of defenses.

So. No story. Nothing happened. No one got hurt, or no more than people do. Everybody got dressed up and went to church, and came back to Erma's house for a great big Sunday dinner, and Bill tickled us and told us not to take any wooden nickels—and I never have—and he was, I do remember now, so very kind. And Spike took me to a burning barn and bribed me, bought my already-willing silence, with a formula for my salvation, once I added in my own, one, slim misunderstanding. It wasn't till I was in high school that I realized that Spike hadn't told me that my mother could go to jail so that I could take on the job of making sure it never happened. Oh, but how strong and capable the misconstruction made me. And how entirely like me, that my strength should be constructed out of little bits of things I took the wrong way.

Now, sitting here tonight, so far away, so close, to all of them, I want to call Erma, at midnight, and say, *Hello, I just remembered you and Bill and Spike and Jessie and everyone,* and I'd be crying in the telephone, and Erma would be puzzled, half-asleep. I've never called her once in fifty years, and Bill's been dead for forty years, and my own mother now has finally gone beyond the reach of any harm. I want to call and bawl my eyes out, I want to reach through the wires and pull them back to me, those people, stand them up in a row and say, *I'll have some answers here,* and fire my questions, show no mercy, screaming out at them, *What happened? How did we, all of us, get lost inside our lives?* And then whisper, soft, in Erma's ear, *Please tell me how, when she was very old, my mother said one time, she never meant to hurt me. Say how she missed me, how she wished I'd never gone away. And tell me how, as she lay dying, that she told you she was setting off to look for me, to find me and to bring me home. Whisper those words softly to me, over and again. And have them be the truth.*

SOMETHING ABOUT THE DARKNESS
SOMETHING ABOUT THE LIGHT

"I JUST WANT TO SHOW YOU WHAT I'M TALKING ABOUT,"
he says, as he precedes me into what has to be the darkest
bedroom in the state of Maine. He crosses the room. "I just
want you to see the kinds of things she wore." She, his dead
wife. Me, a possible replacement. "This is just one closet.
There's more. Far more."

"Any chance of some light?" I say. A half-burnt votive
candle, a boy's flashlight, a bent match. Perhaps a drawn-out
flash of frightening lightning in the summer sky. I am not
particular.

He reaches down and turns on a small, bedside table
lamp, which somehow only serves to illuminate the darkness, to show you just how black and thick it is, and how in-
tractable it very likely will remain. The small, dim lamplight
says, *Okay, look, can you see now: This darkness isn't going
anywhere.*

This man in silhouette slides open a closet door, and I
imagine him pushing a black boulder from the mouth of a
dank cave, where inside, were sufficient light to shine, he
would show me swooping bats and small, imported
wombats, scurrying through a dampness that could penetrate your skin.

"I really can't see," is what I say out loud to him. *You're wigging me out here* is what I really mean.

"Oh sorry," he says, I think betraying that he has spent so much time here in the gloaming that his retinas are retrofitted to the point his vision can pierce now any darkness, make mincemeat of this black, allowing him to look at anything he wants to see.

"Sorry," he says again, a tour guide speaking to an irksome tourist who he hopes will give him a big tip.

He walks over to the window and raises the shade, pulls back heavy draperies to reveal a sunny afternoon just on the far side of the spotty windowpane. But the light meets opposition coming through the glass. The darkness wins, and I turn back to face the closet, let my eyes adjust. I don't want this to be a thing that takes us very long.

"So now you see," he says in a voice that till today I have found gentle to the point of being curative, medicinal and efficacious. A voice that has read Sharon Olds to me on the phone late into the night, that has read George Herbert, Billy Collins, William Butler Yeats, sitting on high, serious rocks along the coast that borders his front lawn.

"So now you see," he says.

And my accommodating eyes are in a clothing store in a big city where so many people could be suited up and dressed for success or for some other money-making enterprise. I see two tiers of suits, jackets, skirts, with blouses demarcating one day's costume from another. Someone has taken pains with the arrangement. No color dares fight with its neighbor. Pinks deepen in tone with subtlety, so that by the time your eyes reach red, they feel as though they have already taken in that color, perhaps only in a different fabric. Although, the fabrics seem not to differ widely from one another. They all appear as though brave fingers would find them every one, soft and smooth, not costly to the touch, however much they set their owner back.

Could not all these have been sold for three hundred dinari and the money given to the poor?

My guide is silent, reverent perhaps. He has brought me here to honor the fashion sense—which I have been told so very much about over the past few weeks—of the woman he spent thirty years with, clothed and unclothed, dressed up, dressing, undressed, redressing. A marriage will be a thing where so much has been put on and taken off so very many times. A marriage will be a thing where none of that protects you on the day the surgeon tells you that what he has discovered cannot be addressed.

This man allows his hand—the same hand that even in a photograph evokes a longing in me—that hand, he allows to slide across the sleeves and cause a rainbow ripple but no sound, no polyester rustle. Hands. If a man knew the things a woman is prepared to forgive of any man whose hands are beautiful, long-fingered, tanned and strong, oh what a knowing that would be. He rests his hand upon one padded shoulder of a jacket, but I think that if I were not here, it would have rested on the silk sleeve of a filmy blouse.

We have not made love. This man and I. I have some good sense, however random its appearance, however unreliable its power to persuade and to hold sway. Oh, but that hand has touched me, in real life and in my sweet imagination. And I have felt things that I have not felt for lifetimes.

We met online—it is where people over fifty meet—where I have met and been met by an architect, a banker, a politician, a physician, and a landscape designer with four trucks and as many current girlfriends. Online. Where I have met twelve sad men. Where each of them has met twelve different, perky women who have sworn blood oaths that they will not be sad again, not if the world ends and if it happens in their kitchen. Sad men, unsaddened women. Juries of our peers. We will indict each other. Rule on guilt and innocence. We are not empanelled to forgive. That much is very clear.

The man has moved now over to a chest of drawers from which he takes a stack of cashmere sweaters. You can see the cashmere from across the room. In the dark. You can hear cashmere.

"Feel these," he says to me, and I walk as though pulled by some long, strong saffron thread to stand across the bed from him and reach down with tired fingers to a space beneath the sweaters. You do not touch cashmere with a palm, or not only in that common way. And I have a fantasy of making love with him laid out and tangled up in piles of cashmere and silk and the kind of cotton born in Egypt, smoothed by water and a sun that they have only there. But that we will not do. Even people who meet pathetically on costly websites will not accost memory in that way. Even people who sleep with four different match-met women at a time do not go there.

"There is no white," he says to me. "Janie did not own one item of clothing that was white. It simply was not her color. It just absolutely was not. And she knew that."

I know that I should leave. I always know that I should leave—from the first sip of tepid coffee that I've paid for myself—at each first meeting. I know that I should look across whatever wobbly table in whatever coffee shop and see what is. I always know that I should get up, excuse myself, mutter something indistinct, and walk away.

This whole enterprise is about that. Deciding when to walk away. The first moment, when you spot him through the window putting money in the parking meter out on the street; the second month, when all your girlfriends say, *You've got to be kidding me*; a year into the thing when one night he says a thing far beyond cruel about a child he fathered before you ever knew that he existed.

It's always about deciding when to leave. Not *if*. *If* is for when you're younger.

The man takes the stack of sweaters, like some impatient store clerk, and puts them gently back into the drawer. I expect him to turn to me and say, *I'm sorry, but we close in fifteen minutes*. But he doesn't. Men don't. Men don't walk away. Or not in my experience. Men are lonely in a way that will not let them.

"Dresses," this man says to me, and snaps his fingers. "Over here." He opens up another closet, taller than the first, and then he turns and for the first time since we walked into the room, he looks, he really looks, at me. He purses his lips, he purses them like a gay man on a TV show, and strokes a beard he doesn't have, then turns back to the closet. And it hits me. It's not darkness is the trouble here. We're blinded by the light. We two are stranded on a desert island in the sun; we neither one like sea or sand. One of us—we can't remember which—has a serious allergy to coconuts. The natives—we don't know how we know—aren't friendly.

He slides the dresses on the hangers down the pole, takes one out, replaces it, and then another. He picks a third and holds it up critically, then turns and holds it out to me.

"This one," he says. "Try this one, first."

FREEING SPIRITS

I WALK THE FEW BLOCKS DOWN TO THE COLLEGE tonight because I read in the paper they were going to free the
souls of a lot of people who were bombed at Hiroshima. The
paper said they were going to put the souls in little paper
lanterns holding lighted candles, and when they floated on
the water this would let the troubled spirits finally float free.
I'm thinking that if it's that simple, why didn't they do it
sixty years ago?

Turns out there's a reason. That's the thing about life.
There's so often a reason. It seems that a soul has to hover
sixty years first, in order for the thing to work. Personally,
I'm pretty skeptical of any religion that has much to do with
the whole numbers thing. Personally, I'm pretty skeptical of
any religion. Though I have to say that once the Buddhist
priest starts crooning and half the hundred-and-forty-seven
people on the boathouse dock croon too and I look up and
see the several clouds and feel the bits of wind that ripple
tiny riffs across the water, my skepticism melts in the heat of
the hundred-and-forty-six lighted candles—I ever the ab-
stainer. What? Am I fearful if I light a candle I may inad-
vertently join some church? But my skepticism melts in the
heat of all the bodies crooning, being crooned at. It takes
very little actually to dynamite a person's unbelief. We all sit

poised to topple over at the first little cataclysmic miracle.
We walk around all day looking to be duped, healed, made
whole and holy and transformed.

The Buddhist priest—if so he is—decked out in red and
yellow says that now he will pray for us, though he neglects
to say to whom. I want to raise my hand at the Q & A and
say *To whom?* using the objective case, though I object to
hardly any prayer. I want to ask: *To whom did you pray for us
tonight?* hoping he will tell me to the god who made the
dark-skinned, black-eyed child who dances in a long, bright
fuchsia dress, just at the edge of the boat dock, the god who
will be with her till the hour of her death—ideally not tonight, if her smiling mother has the presence of mind to
jump in after her when she falls off the edge, and does not
make her wait the mandatory sixty years. (Try to tell a story
without numbers in it. Try to make religion number-free.)

The priest/monk finishes his intonation and hands the
mike off to a woman of the sort who is so often given to
holding microphones on boat docks and passing out petitions and saying in a voice amplified beyond necessity that
all the mayors in Western Massachusetts have signed a declaration saying they are in favor of peace. She is a stocky
woman, given to saying this, and other things not unlike
this, into a microphone designed for karaoke. She speaks
with a straight face. I make no comment here. I have my
hands full with the facts.

Then someone reads a poem that I think must certainly
regret its own having been written, much less read aloud,
with people present. Then someone reads a letter from a

woman who was bombed at Hiroshima as a child, bombed—at least her body was and bore the nuclear aberrations thereby instituted there. We bombed her body, though I think not her spirit, judging from the letter. It is her mother and her father and her sisters and her brothers, thousands of them, we are come to free the spirits of tonight. A woman reads this letter and we're done for, and there is no Buddhist god can save us from our sins. We are Americans.

I write with a woman by the name of Jasmine. Every Thursday night we sit and write together. It's the sort of thing that people in my neighborhood are prone to do. This summer Jasmine is working as a teacher with a migrant project and she writes about the children, children with so many languages, though none that speak in any voice that's audible outside the ghettos where they go to sleep, a dozen to a room, the temperature inside the black night place no more than four degrees lower than the temperature out in the noonday field, where one boy in the class refused the Popsicle he was offered in his worry for his pregnant mother who he thought would have a baby in the field that afternoon, and maybe die.

Jasmine writes about the children's languages and about the one little girl who has no language, none at all, who never speaks, has never spoken, if Jasmine understands the Mayan English the brother tells the story in.

Jasmine writes about the boy who offers the class his death-won metaphor when she is teaching the children about similes—the things that are important—and asking for examples. He says, "The dessert is an invisible monster who kills people. I think that is a simile, if it is not a metaphor," and tells her then about the people he saw die. And Jasmine says that if the current legislation now in committee ever makes it out, it will be not a felony, but only a misdemeanor for a teacher who does not report any child who is in this *ohbeautifulforspaciousskies* country of ours without his proper papers.

As though we would, any of us, be here had such papers of *our* people been required. We are all without papers, and until we know that fact we are all well and truly damned. Jasmine says the proposed legislation will mean that buses will go town to town rounding up the aliens—a word which once meant men from Mars. The buses will drive straight through the middle of families, splitting them apart, likely for all time.

Jasmine says she took a used TV and an old VCR to the family of the little girl who does not speak. Five strong men would not let Jasmine in, but took the TV and a fourteen-year-old computer someone had sent along, and they said *thank you thank you thank you,* a hundred different times.

Then tomorrow she says she is taking them a stack of videos—*age appropriate*—and I say, "Jasmine, do they have a car to carry these things when they move with the seasons to the South?" and she says no, and I say, "Do they have a place to live there, a socket in a wall to plug the VCR into? A wall?" and she says no and I say, "What will they do with these things?" and she says, "I don't know."

And Jasmine is the one who's helping. This summer she is the only person in America who gets into a car and drives a fourteen-year-old computer to this neighborhood where God's afraid to go.

The woman with the microphone instructs the yellow-and-red-robed, bald Buddhist priests to light the candles in the lanterns now and tells a tanned, athletic-looking woman in a kayak to row gently as she starts to pull the lanterns fastened onto tiny platforms made of styrofoam all tied together, out across the pond. She says again—I guess in case we didn't read it in the paper, or we forgot—that now the spirits of the people that we killed can all go free.

MY BOOK GROUP:
WARS AND DYING

THIS IS WHAT THE WORLD HAS COME TO: BOOK GROUPS. Tonight, in mine, what's following the chocolate mousse with brandied berries and stiffly whipped, cream-colored cream is: "What do you remember about the war?" The war in question, WWII.

Reading a new book each month is really overkill. No matter what we read we use as an excuse to sit in a circle and talk about ourselves.

So. Ourselves and WWII. Another night it might be ourselves and recycling.

Jane Francis goes first. Jane always goes first.

"Well. I can remember sitting in the shadows," she says, "nights when my big sisters brought their boyfriends home. This would have been, oh, I don't know, 1946 or '47, and one boy my sister Nancy knew was from France. He said when he was just fourteen that he and two friends would kill German soldiers. No weapons, no noise, they'd jump a soldier on patrol, and stifle and then smother him." Jane shudders for effect. "He said three boys could take one soldier easily. They did it over and again. He mentioned it so casually. I want to say his name was Ralph, can that be right?"

Leah Roth gets up and moves from her chair over to the window seat. Mean pain is on her face. It's in her eyes.

"Are you okay?" Polly says.

Leah waves her hand.

"Shall I go next?" Anne says. She looks slightly terrified. Dying scares her to death. "Okay, then. Well, while my father was at war, we lived with my mother and my sisters and my grandmother and aunts, all in one house together, and I was so very happy, and then my father came home. He took us off to live in a dingy apartment in Pittsburgh, and I hated it. I hated him. I missed my life. He never talked about the war. He never did. The only story he ever told was about one night when he went to the latrine, passing a soldier on the way, and while he was inside he heard a terrible yelp and moan and ugly groaning, and he came outside, and the soldier lay dead, strangled by a boa constrictor. That was in Burma. That is the only story that he ever told."

Leah pushes herself up from the window seat and moves to stand behind an empty Windsor chair. She waves off the question no one asks, and we forbear to catch one another's eye. We know there's nothing we can do.

"My father was thirty-six. Old then." Sally speaks spitfire, not even waiting for the yelp groan moan of the boa constrictor's victim to fade. "He was thirty-six and he had five young sons, and he believed that if the war was legitimate enough to send poor young men to die, then it was legitimate enough for him to volunteer. He died at sea. He took a piece of shrapnel in the arm, a little piece, but it became infected, and he got pneumonia. There was no penicillin on the ship. It would have cured him."

"At what age?" I say.

"He was thirty-six."

"No, I mean, what age were you?"

"Seven."

I pour more tea and try to decide if I think that explains a lot. I am forever trying to make life offer reasons.

Just before my turn comes, I'll run into the loo. My eighteen-year-old father enlisted in the Navy and was discharged after six months time for walking in his sleep. *Not a good thing on board a ship* was always the standard finish to the story—as though battleships were flat platforms with no sides, with decks strewn with snoring sailors who might slide off in slumber or in catnaps sleepwalk into the sea.

Or, I could sit here and say my father's best friend Tommy Nelson was killed at Normandy, and that my dad gave Tommy's mother a brand new leather pocketbook for Mother's Day each May till 1987, with a card he signed *Love, Tommy.*

"My father came home," Becky says. Her words are tentative, almost apologetic. "My little sister had died while he was away. Once he came home I followed him everywhere. I wouldn't let him out of my sight."

Leah moves suddenly and says she's sorry but she needs to leave, time for her meds. Polly grabs her coat and says she'll drive Leah home. They leave quickly. We all make a big project of saying goodnight. Leah is dying, soon, her cancer back for the third and final knock-out round.

But there is nothing we cannot ignore. It's what we do. We forget together. We pretend. We damn ocean tides to keep from any knowing we can't handle. We know too much already. It's why we live the lives we do.

"My cousin's father grew up in Holland." Molly speaks softly. Every sentence said tonight has about six jobs to do. "He tells us stories of their having to build German airplanes, of their building them designed to crash. He tells of hiding in the closet with his brother the night they came to houses to round up young men to go as soldiers to the front."

"Bullshit!" is what my friend Dick Goldman will say later when I tell him all these stories. "This is the sort of crap made up to hide the fact that everyone stood by and didn't do a single damn thing to stop the slaughter."

Now the memories tumble out. It seems not to matter which woman tells which one, for I cannot seem to make the stories fit the tellers. A couple of the women say how their fathers liked the camaraderie and how they thrived on having important work to do with other men.

War is not a book group.

We talk on until finally the room is all filled up with bodies and war stories and dead men—for all the fathers, who lived through the unlivable and came home to live such ordinary lives, are now dead. And everyone who's in the room tonight is going to die, and there is that flat place in the conversation that says that everybody for a moment knows that.

"We haven't said what we will read next time," Jane says, as though it might save even one life. "What should we read next time?"

Lots of suggestions are offered, and then Anne, who was angry that her father came back from the war, says—as far as I can figure, apropos of nothing—"I have been wondering what if we as a group could become more political or something?" This is followed by a flurry of suggestions of books we could read about greenhouse gases and sex slaves and fuel emissions, and the conversation degenerates to politics, and everyone agrees the wars in Iraq and Afghanistan should end, and Becky timidly says that we somehow think the lives of the students who were slain at Virginia Tech or Columbine are worth more than the lives of the Afghans we are killing every day.

We should do something.

A declaration so often met with suggestions of bake sales and rallies and marches and sit-ins. Once even, in this very group, with the idea of a naked carwash to raise money for some cause. *People would pay us to put our clothes back on.* We, the aging, wrinkled children of the men, good men, husbands, fathers, who for us fought and died.

We hear the back door open, and Leah all but stumbles into the room. Polly follows close behind. "Leah wanted to come back," she says.

"I can't die," Leah says. Her words are feathers. She sinks into a chair. "I have to die. I can't."

We are no longer breathing.

"The war," Leah says. "The question." She inhales and seems to breathe in strength. "The war … my father."

Auschwitz? Buchenwald? A car drives by the house. The headlight flashes in the window, sweeps the aging faces.

"Nazi." Leah speaks the single word, demanding that it stand there alone and trample all the other words who might rise in contention. "Nazi," Leah says again. "I know it."

Jane makes a purring sound. Leah shakes her head and scowls.

"Know it," she says.

Anne moves to stand behind Leah's chair, then, bending over, puts her head down on Leah's shoulder. All the color leaves Leah face. She slumps and we all jump up and together move Leah to the sofa.

"Shall I call her doctor?" Polly says.

"No." Leah's eyes open slowly. "Not…."

"Should we drive you to the hospital?" Pauline says.

"No," Leah says. "Just heavy." She closes her eyes. Her breathing doesn't sound right.

"Do you want a pillow?" I say.

No answer. Polly scowls at me.

"My whole life," Leah speaks softly now, but evenly. "I couldn't."

A log falls in the fire, an artificial, crinkly sound.

"My mother," Leah says. "I did not forgive her."

"There is nothing to forgive," Jane says.

Leah exhales a puff of pure, disgusted air.

"I think we should call someone," Anne says.

"No mercy," Leah says. Her words are garbled now, though the meaning is clearer, if anything. "Forgive me."

"We forgive you," Anne says, her words more stupid than Jane's negation of any need for forgiveness. "Do you want us to call a rabbi," I say. I almost said, a priest.

Leah waves her hand, impatient. "Pay," she says.

We every blessed one of us wonder is she saying *Pray*. And I believe that if we could, we would.

"Sing," Leah says, her voice a little whisper now, an ugly whisper, flinging random orders to the night.

We look at each other.

"I think she wants us to sing," Anne says.

When we spent a weekend at the Cape last summer, we made a bonfire on the beach, as it was getting dark, and we sang together: *Kumbaya. This Land is Your Land,* and *Breaking Up is Hard to Do.* It was late and finally very dark. We were the only people on the sand, the only people on the earth. And every time we stopped to pick another song, there was the sound of small waves breaking, over and again, drawn by a moon not one of us could see.

I don't know any Jewish songs to sing to someone who is dying. And in fact what does start playing in my head is an old hymn, "Softly and Tenderly Jesus is Calling," a song imprinted on my brain in some other, now long-distant lifetime.

I am back in church in Marksville, Ohio, and Doris Dolby at the piano is plunking out the verses like she means never to stop. The service has been going on for days. But there is no Jesus, soft and tender, here. No Jesus—or if there is, he is small and soft and brown and no match for God, who's made of equal parts of white lightning ire and purple thunder. I hear the rail-thin, shiny-black-suited preacher rail. He has one sermon, as I remember it, and he preaches it on Sunday night. In my so-churched childhood, it is always Sunday night, and someone is always going to hell before the night is over. On far too many childhood Sunday nights, I am afraid that someone will be me.

One sermon, preached in one black suit: *Be very sure your sins will find you out. Tonight thy soul may be required of thee.*

So at about the age of five, I started to get saved. I went forward to the altar, every week, hell-bent on repenting sins I hadn't been alive long enough to have committed. The big voices, the big people—all surrounding me and using up the air I might have used to breathe—singing:

> Just as I am without one plea
> but that thy blood was shed for me
> and that thou bidst me come to thee,
> oh Lamb of God, I come.

And then later—long, life hours later:

> Softly and tenderly Jesus is calling,
> calling oh sinner come home,
> see on the portals he's waiting and watching,
> watching for you and for me.

Nice words really. Whispered images. Hardly scary at all. But the song came too late in the evening. The damage had been done, the photographs of hell projected on the ceiling and the walls and on my brain. The sweet words, the soft music no match for damnation. I went up to the altar, knelt at the rail, which hit me at forehead height, and waited, crying, waited until the singing would be done and the Sunday School Superintendent would come and kneel beside me to pray. He, a large man who scared me only slightly less than what awaited me if I did not kneel here, every Sunday night forever—until my mother set me straight.

"It's wonderful that you go forward," she said. *Go forward*. Such a puny euphemism for the walk down that aisle, weekly wondering if I was going to faint, or maybe only die. "It's wonderful that you go forward, only, not every week."

I couldn't even *get saved* right. Her words made me feel greedy, inappropriate. The feeling is there to this day, to be resurrected even now: whenever I must speak in public, whenever I stand anywhere I might be seen.

Can it be there is a difference between who God is and what people do? If an arsonist dumps gallons of gasoline on your upholstered furniture and lights a match and burns your house down to the ground, must you not tremble every time you put gas in your car? Is gasoline not gasoline? Is God not Earle Watson?

Go back to the church. The service this summer Sunday night will last straight through to eternity, and I have to pee. I signal to my mother and I leave the pew and then the building. You have to walk either to the front of the sanctuary and open the small, loud door at the side of the altar rail, or else go outside and walk around the building, which I always do, no matter if it's pouring rain. I close the church door and turn and there is Lou Cohen. He's one of about three Jews in our town and the only one I really know. The music is pouring through the open transom windows all around, people clinging to the *Old Rugged Cross* for dear life. Lou says hello and asks me what the song is. I tell him I don't know. I ask him if he wrote his Africa report for Mrs. Wilson tomorrow. He tells me no, but he will get it done. He does not mention that he will grow up and one day live in Africa, and marry there and father four fine sons. He does ask me though if I know who killed Jesus. I tell him I'm not sure. We say good night.

Lou's on my mind tonight as I sit silent with the others, watching Leah who has now fallen fast asleep, her breath now strong and loud. Lou's on my mind because he called me, no more than a week ago. We hadn't spoken in I bet twenty years. It was Boxing Day, December 26, and I was making short work of dismantling the Christmas tree— never a big fan of the whole *boughs of holly* thing—when the phone rang.

It was Lou—or so the man whose gravel voice I would not have recognized would have me to believe. Lou, who dispensed with the intervening years by sleight of hand, and without ceremony or excuse, plowed into the story of his life. I said something like *How are you?* and he told me his life story. The whole thing.

Now please remember, I was daily present for all that mattered of thirteen of the first eighteen years of the life in question, daily present, dully unaware.

Unaware that at the age of five, Lou moved to a new house and the first afternoon the neighborhood boys called him to come out to play and led him to a tree, well out of sight of any savior, to grab and tie him to the trunk and crumble newspaper with bark and twigs to set on fire, to burn Lou at the stake. As punishment. For killing Jesus.

A neighbor hanging out the laundry next door smelled smoke and ran to halt the execution.

Lou told me he was beaten up on a reliable, anticipatable basis for the next twelve years.

As punishment.

For killing Jesus.

At one point in adolescence, he said, he convinced his parents to let him transfer to the Catholic high school in town, the paradoxical protection there arising from the fact that Catholics—no, give them their confirmation names: *Spic, Mick, Pollack, Dago*—were so beleaguered by the bigots in the town, they had no time or heart for pummeling or burning at the stake some *Kike*, although this was not the word the *Spic/Mick/Polack/Dago* kids would use for Lou, who was supposed to have crucified the Virgin Mary's Holy Son.

But, Lou told me, not pausing for a breath, his troubles started long before his Joan of Arc encounter with the Christians neighbor boys. When Lou was three years old, his mother in a fit of fury, reached out and slapped his face as he sat in the antique, clawfoot bathtub filled halfway to the top with cooling water. Lou hadn't washed behind his ears, his mother hit him hard enough to send him sprawling, and his head went under. It took a lifetime for Lou to push against the weight of heavy hand, to gasping grab onto the curled rim of the bathtub and to breathe. Alone then in the room.

Some days later—Lou would live to verify the exact date on the certificate of death, but will never know the interval of time between the two events—Lou's mother put his baby sister in the bathtub and told Lou to watch her. He leaned over the edge of the big tub and grabbed onto the baby's arm—he does not name her in this telling, but in my heart I must believe she had a name, this soul inside that soft, soap-slippery body Lou lost hold of. (*Did she squirm and splash? Did Lou sneeze?* No one living knows.) I do know, because he told me, that not one bit of this did he remember till the age of forty-five; Lou, then a physician of some renown, sitting at a table at an international convention of world experts on child abuse, a thing Lou spent most of his grown-up years avenging.

Life had stolen memory. Those days were. Then they were made to not have been. Lou's family never mentioned his sister's death, not one time in all the years that followed. The family moved to a new town, leaving history bound and gagged behind.

Then Lou, sitting in a meeting, in one blinding flash remembered everything, and he died. The memory murdered him, as it would do. And when he came to life again, not all of him came too. And so, he said, he has been limping, dragging, crying tearless, quiet cries that turn to rocks inside when they are swallowed. And he has been successful; his career has been the stuff of wide acclaim; he's made life easier to live for more people than most people meet in any lifetime. And he has lived for the past thirty years with a woman who is astonishingly beautiful, he has raised four sons, and every day life forces him to come up with a new reason not to kill himself. Life wants a brand new, different reason every morning.

And there I sat last Saturday, the cold New England sunlight pouring through the window, the spoils of Christmas everywhere, Lou's whole life laid out there on the coffee table beside the Christmas decorations and the teakwood crèche, and only then I noticed that the baby Jesus was nowhere in sight. The wobbly manger stood, the shepherds' crooks prepared to hold them up forever, Joseph and Mary looking like they could stand all night supported by their floor-length skirts, the single angel lying, white wings locked for flight, lame, awkward, grounded, on his side.

Lou told me about Buddha and his meditation practice, this, on the heels of his flirtation with religions I had never heard of. He spoke of his yoga, his dope, his gym, his vitamins, his trainer, as I rifled frantically through piles of toy drums and snowflakes, candy canes and twinkle lights, to find the baby Jesus. Lou said he went to Peru last summer to a healing mountain where he smoked some dope and entered some strange states of consciousness. I got down on my hands and knees to see if perhaps the Christ Child had fallen beneath the sofa. Lou said it helped him for awhile. But, he said, it was not helping now. I stood up, and there half buried in a bowl of hard tack candy was the baby Jesus. He was sticky, with lint clinging to him, and he was not even teakwood, but plastic.

My Book Group: Wars and Dying

My friend Sally tells me of a concentration camp survivor who says, *Say nothing about God you cannot say standing over a pit filled with the bodies of dead children.*

This tiny, plastic Jesus would not answer.

But oh, I wished that afternoon there was some other Jesus. Some Jesus who could well and truly save us from all the dying done back then, from all the dying we do every day now. Some Jesus who might pull the bodies of the fist-fighting, fire-setting boys off their pummeling pile and get them to stand over in the corner, line them up and say to Lou, *Look here. Look at these boys, they are not me, I do not know them, we have never met.*

Ah, but then we would need to talk about where Jesus was on the afternoon Lou's mother saw her little boy's head a murky shadow in the cloudy water of the tub and bent to put her hand on him, then walked out of the room. We would need more information regarding Jesus' whereabouts when that same woman left that little boy, that little girl—to lose hold, to slip from tiny fingers—to slip from living, from *this* living, both of them. A savior's torture must be made to answer that. Lou's story wants more than sacrifice; it wants redressing, resurrection, because if all that is on offer is a dead Jesus, it isn't worth whatever Verizon is charging for the phone call.

If there is no Jesus well and truly risen from the dead, then we will have to go scour the Midwest for a gang of middle-aged guys in golf shirts—a bunch of guys who were awful when they were kids and who are awful still—and fly down to Florida to hold a pillow over the face of a now-ancient, senile mother, lost for decades in asylum, then go knock on doors of sleeping judges, juries, court reporters; call them to the court of final say. Who is guilty? (Any old psych textbook you buy for fifty cents at a yard sale will tell you a young child would rather damn himself than damn his mother: if she is a demon, he is lost.) Who pays for this crime? (A baby did. A girl, a woman, she might have grown to be. Let us decide we will not think of her.) Who else must pay? How much? How long? Until the jury rules, Lou will have to smoke more dope, and sleep with far more women and chant and pray and do another hundred thousand more good deeds, and exercise until his muscles take on muscles of their own. And every morning he will need to come up with one more reason to go on living—maybe not as good as yesterday's, but good enough—until the day no reason comes to him.

Jesus will be up to this, or Jesus is not interesting at all.

I must have been humming under my breath, because Jane nods.

"I remember that," she says and starts to hum with me softly.

"Sing," Leah says, still groggy.

Jane and I, obedient, begin to hum the song more loudly:

> Softly and tenderly Jesus is calling,
> calling for you and for me,
> see on the portals he's waiting and watching,
> watching for you and for me.

Sally joins in, then Becky in low harmony. We are of an age and of a history—however long-denied—that bequeath not only all the songs from World War II, but tune and lyric of old warhorse hymns, camp-meeting songs our grandmothers rocked us to.

Our humming now is strong and certain.

We hear the back door again. *The Angel of Death*, I think. But it's Becky's husband, just back from a trip. He walks in, cued by the humming to be silent, and sees Leah lying far too still now on the sofa.

"Is she okay?" He whispers.

No, we all shake our heads.

"Words," Leah says, her voice now odd and raspy.

We all look at one another.

We stand, still humming on, playing the words over in our heads:

> Come home, come home,
> you who are weary, come home;
> earnestly, tenderly, Jesus is calling,
> calling, O sinner, come home.

"Words," Leah says clearly. "Sing words."
And so we do.

> Why should we linger and heed not His mercies;
> time is now fleeting, the moments are passing;
> shadows are gathering, deathbeds are coming,
> coming for you and for me;
> *t*hough we have sinned, He has mercy and pardon,
> pardon for you and for me.

We sing, but we are not full-throated—give us that. Our friend is dying, on a weeknight, at a book group, but we are smart women, the ones who read, who snicker at salvation. We sing hymns, but we are posing. This is masquerade, charade, some sentimental caricature of what we will not be believing, not ever.

Let some stern woman stomp her foot.

Any comfort needed, we can and will invent. We, the daughters of the men who long since fought and died so that we might craft our own salvation. No, even that, we don't believe. No one dies for anybody else. *Don't die for me.*

No. If we sing old hymns tonight, we will be wry and properly ironic when we speak of it tomorrow.

If tonight we sing old savior songs, well, we will grimace when we tell the story; we will shake our heads and say just what a funny thing life is.

It's seldom we're in any danger: like on the telephone with Lou on Boxing day; like on the summer's night when he and I, the children, stood outside that church, so close we could reach out and touch some other story; like tonight, when just for one brief terrifying moment, in a room grown colder, in peculiar light, some Savior stands, all bold and bloodied, threatening to die again this late in the proceedings to save us from our sins, he says: to make this lifetime, when all is said and done and well and truly ended, seem like a night in a bad hotel, like a dream we have awakened from to hear our mother downstairs in the kitchen, making breakfast, calling us to come, as though the years had never been.

We will not have it.

Leah lies here on the sofa, her breath more shallow, but still even.

"She looks so peaceful," Polly says.

"Polly, you're an ass," no holy prophet of our number says back in return. Polly's words are what we've got, they are what we have signed up to believe. We are women of integrity. *To cease to be* is what peace is, and there is no forgiveness; we need none, no savior, no salvation. Death is a flat line on a monitor, and if there is a torment in the dying, well, we're okay with that. Our comfort is obliteration. Our peace: annihilation.

"That Nazi," Anne says. "That horrible monster that must have raped Leah's mother."

Ah. Yes.

"What God would stand by and watch that?" Jane says.

We're almost fine. In another minute we will have moved from a dying woman calling out on the last night of her life for mercy, to our long-practiced scorn.

We have these close calls, but we survive. It isn't hard—in fact, it actually gets easier—to wave the pain of living in God's face and make him disappear. As long as we've got earnest, skinny preachers in black suits preaching hellfire and damnation, and booted Nazis, and bully schoolboys who burn up the neighbor children, we will be all right. As long as longing can be crucified—that work of life's late afternoon—we will be fine.

WALKING BY THE RECTORY

I'M BACK IN MY HOMETOWN, in fact or in imagination. The distinction is not always clear. It's late and cold and dark, and it's December, and as I scurry by St. Andrews and look up at the gold-colored cross, it occurs to me that I have somehow misplaced thirty years. I frown at the darkened, leaden windows and realize I can account for maybe half my life.

I never linger passing any Catholic church. We, who grew up as frank Baptists, thinking priests Rome clones whose old, worn-shiny black robes were infested with the dust of papal-blackened magic, always scurried by. Priests were a bit alarming, but at least you never saw one on the street. They did not frequent public thoroughfares, but lived in ancient, eighteen-room rectories made of brick, or stone, or some fortress-fit material, kept clean and warm by a devout and stern, bone-thin Irish/Italian woman who cooked outrageous dinners of roast beef, and roast potatoes, and other roasted things, and cakes with rum and brandy as the main ingredients.

The rectories had standard-issue table lamps placed dead center in front of every window, so that walking by in half light, half shivers, half hunger, half despair, the place looked the very picture of a heaven a person might well have some interest in. Those yellow lights dredged longing from your protesting soul for never-visited, forgotten, still-remembered things. That's what the lights were for, to make you long to be a Catholic in a thick, warm coat with thick, warm soup steaming on the stove and smelling of the tartest tarragon, with the heartiest potatoes, capable of holding their own with savory meat and ripe, perspiring cheese, and powerful brown bread, to be washed down with overflowing flasks of purple, grape communion wine. Lights like that could make a person go to catechism five afternoons a week.

I walked by this rectory two times a day for all the years that memory was occupied with casting things in stone, and the edifice did not fail, not one time, to capture my attention.

I walk on by in failing light tonight, and think I will avert my eyes in passing by the rectory. But it's no good. The bricks are magnetized. They'd draw my gaze if I were blind. I study the structure like a puzzle it will be to my sincere advantage to decipher. I stop, arrested by a little, cold-sounding, noisy click, exaggerated by the holy silence that the night forbears to break, now settling down around the holy house.

A priest walks out on the front porch. He bends to pick up the newspaper. I would have thought a priest would have a housekeeper to bring the paper in, unfold it, press it, maybe with an iron. On low. No steam.

When I was a child, if a priest needed a pocket comb or razor blades, he never went himself, but sent a nun to do the shopping. I am assuming here, but how else explain the frequent sightings of nuns, who with unsettling regularity cruised the aisles of five-and-tens and pharmacies, so that you never were entirlely free of the possibility of them.

Their long black habits, their sad, if contented, faces, I found menacing in ways a burly priest could never be. I knew these priests could not boil water for their tea, nor darn the holes in holy socks nor in their love-made, wooly sweaters; whereas, even children, such as I, who were Protestant enough to go to church three times a week—to go to hell, if it should come to that—knew nuns were capable of anything. Even I, who could only tell for certain who was Catholic and who was not by looking at their saddle oxford shoes—black and white sold just to Protestants, brown and white to baptized members of the holy Roman Mother Church—knew nuns were somehow fierce and capable beyond all reason. I wanted nothing to do with them and was always more than reassured to see the woman hanging out the sheets beside the rectory was not done up like any bride of Christ in thin, black, silky clothes.

I think if the Grim Reaper with his hooded cloak and ample scythe is the very picture of death, then nuns in pairs or triplets in the middle aisle of the five-and-ten were mystery made manifest, something *other,* dressed in black, with well-hidden hair, unrouged skin, unpainted lips, and pale-lashed eyes.

I give a little shudder. The priest holding the newspaper on the porch in the December night turns and lifts the creaky mailbox lid to take out one slim bit of mail, perhaps a letter from another priest who's lost his faith—the second time this year—perhaps only a reminder from his dentist (this assuming priests have teeth in need of care).

He looks down the letter and then raises his eyes and stares out at the night.

Just in case.

He lifts his chin.

Dear God in Heaven. Holy Mary Mother of God, I would say if I were Catholic. It's David Thomas, or if it's not, it is a balding priest whose got his face.

David Thomas, Dave Tom. Davey Tommy. Wavey Davey. Tom the Bomb. I went to school with him. We went to the same church—a hundred days a week—the same Baptist church that fervently and vocally believed the only worse thing than the devil was the Pope. We had it straight from John, that first and most emphatic Baptist. The only people that we knew for sure were going to hell were Catholics.

So how did Davey Thomas catapult his eternally saved self from the water tank beneath our altar at First Baptist to the Holy Roman Church, and not just as a casual convert, but as a well-nourished man of the cloth, complete with collar, black clothes, and a twelve-room rectory?

"Hello," he calls out. Even his voice is Davey Thomas's.

I start, and realize I've been standing, frozen, freezing, in one spot, and staring. I'm not infrequently surprised to tune back in and discover what my body has been up to while my mind has been off on a Disney cruise. It doesn't worry me; I always feel the slightest bit invisible. One of life's watchers, never a watched one.

"Hello," I say softly enough to leave my options open. We study one another.

At least he doesn't ask if he can help me. He hasn't grown that pompous yet.

"I like December," he calls out.

I hate it. Not the month itself, only the Christmas part, which does all but hog the whole thing.

"Your mother loved December," I say, still softly.

"What?" he says as he starts down the stairs, each careful step assuring me I need not raise my voice, that he will come as close as need be. I can whisper if I want.

"Your mother loved December," I say again.

"I know," he says, "And your mum despised it. In fact, I can't remember a month she did like."

"You recognize me." I am surprised. I had my nose fixed in my twenties, and my acne's gone. I've put on thirty needless pounds and had my teeth capped, and my hair is a new, close-cropped strawberry blond—fruit red in certain light.

"Of course, I recognize you. I'm a priest, not an idiot."

I'd be a whole lot less surprised were it the other way around.

So how did it happen? I want to ask, but I can't get from where I am, to any phrasing short of cheeky rude. How on earth did they ever let a Baptist be a priest? *What possessed them?* My mother would have said. In my mother's book, you stuck to your own kind and everybody knew where everybody was. A Baptist priest, no use to them, and none to his own people.

He points to his dog collar like he's shooting it. "You're probably wondering where I got these clothes."

"I figured Rome," I say.

"VaticanGarb.com."

That's another thing about a Catholic. They're so precise.

"You're cold out here," Davey says. "Come in." He points to the holy fortress and does a little jig-jog step, and we are seven-year-old kids, double-dog daring one another up the walk, with taunts and jibes and shrieks and shoves. *"I dare you." "I double dare you." "Pope, Pope on a rope." "Nuns, nuns, they have guns."* Until finally, emboldened by the darkness and the cold that in the end is only wearying, we grab hands and run together up and touch the railing on the porch, then turn and run till we are heaving, out of breath, and later on at night, will lie awake and wonder—long after all the nuns in town are fast asleep—wonder is it possible we have contracted some papal disease, committed some unpardonable, Protestant sin? We're not afraid of Catholic punishment for our "trespasses"—which only they and Presbyterians, and certain Methodists, implore "Our Father" to "forgive." Baptists pray forgive us our "debts" as we forgive our "debtors," and would be entirely satisfied with that. We're not afraid of *them*. We are afraid of *us*. "Don't tell the preacher," we whisper to each other the next day in the yard at school.

"Come in," Davey says. "Come on in."

"We can't," I say. "I mean, I can't. You can't be bringing women in."

"I'm not about to *have my way* with you. I'm offering you a cup of tea, or sherry, unless that's still a sin."

"No, sherry's fine."

"Well, come then. I'll show you around."

What? Doesn't he know what he's doing? Can he not remember? He stands here, on this Wednesday, in old, cold December, and he threatens to fulfill a wish I've carried around alive with me for fifty years.

Come in, he says, just like that. *Here, have a million dollars. Here, be twenty-two again and three full inches taller. Here, marry this movie star we have for you.*

I move on stick-stiff legs with Davey up the walk. I'm going to my coronation. The audience has clapped the loudest and the longest for my story. I'm *Queen for a Day*. I am condemned. My legs now carry me, against my will, to my certain execution.

Davey pulls open the heavy door—I think perhaps a bit self-consciously, but I'm in no state to judge, when at the moment, I could well mistake a flicker for a bolt of lightning.

"Here, let me take your coat," Davey says.

I need it, it's holding me together, I don't say. "I can only stay for a minute," I say instead.

Somehow I would have expected to be greeted by a parlor maid, petite, decked out in art-deco-age black rayon, under a white, complicated apron, wearing a white frilly cap. But, we are quite alone.

I'd like to stand here, in this foyer for an hour, take it in, then come back every afternoon and do a different room. At the same time I would like to run from room to room like a crazy person, panting, gushing, slipping on the Catholic, oriental rugs. I'd like to go back home and get my stuff and move right in and stay forever. Davey could sneak me in and out at night for exercise. I could grow old and die here and the tinted ochre walls would never tell. Davey and I could drive to West Virginia after years of long companionship—if not desire—and marry, make it all right in the sight of God, if not the Catholic Church. The two are not the same. But you knew that.

Alternatively, I could run out to the pantry, trip the housekeeper as she crosses the kitchen carrying six ramekins of custard in a pan of boiling water from the oven to the counter, and then visit her daily in the burn ward of the local hospital and take her job as penance—something Baptists are more practiced at than might be generally believed.

Or, they might discharge the housekeeper from the Catholic hospital, scars healed and hardly showing. It would be a miracle. And I could come and live here, not to wash and iron and scrub, but to be washed and ironed and scrubbed for.

"What would you like to see first?" Davey says.

"The cellar." My honest reply. It's a matter of not wanting the best too soon. It's eating the crust before the filling; aging a new dress in the closet for six months; getting all As for sixteen years in a row before you take a day off school to watch two movies.

"I don't recommend the basement," Davey says. "Lots of little rooms that must have once been torture chambers during the Midwest inquisition, not to mention noisy plumbing, dust, and mice."

Davey leads me room to room. He's nine years old and showing me his castle, sneaking peeks to see my wonderment. That, or I am lying sprawled across his narrow twin bed, in the sorry room he shares with his twin sister, Julie Ann—my best friend—while he's out playing stick ball. We girls lie here planning lives that are far, far too big for anybody from this town. This bedroom, their whole house, is a nightmare. Even the preacher's wife says somebody should torch the thing and start again, and she is generally thought to be a most resourceful woman. Davey and Julie Ann's mother, who once had a *nervous breakdown*, lies on the davenport downstairs, while rampant clutter and a sad disorder overrun the place.

Julie Ann has a small beat-up bureau she keeps tidy, with a limp doily weighted with a jewelry box—home to a wounded ballerina—with a King James Bible lying on the top. But it's an aberration in this musty-smelling house, where misery and grime have won the battle long ago.

Each room Davey shows me is pristine in twelve beautiful and different ways. It may be the one experience of my life that offers me no disappointment. It is a Catholic house in the same way the house where Davey and Julie Ann grew up was Baptist, pure and simple, far beyond human redemption, dependent entirely and forever on the grace of God and Jesus' mercy. This rectory is self-sufficient. It hardly needs a God at all. Its walls are sturdy, flanked by cherry hardwood worn to rich patina. It is a house to run to in the storm.

Not quite the house where you grew up, I want to say to Davey, but something happens when you turn eighteen that makes that sort of sentence stop at your puckered lips, all phrased to pose, but never spoken.

"You live here all alone?" I say.

"I know. I know," he says. "You're thinking people sleep out on the street, and I have fourteen rooms." It's obvious he's counted. "Not a heck of a whole lot like the place where we grew up."

Heck. That's Baptist. A born Catholic would say *hell*, or not say anything.

"Whatever happened to Julie Ann?" I say.

"Nothing happened." He speaks like that's my fault. "She still lives over in the flats. She has five kids, and a hundred grandkids, and a husband that's a wicked drunk."

I do not think it ever once occurred to me, sprawled out on Davey's wire-spring bed, daydreaming in concert with Julie Ann, that she and Davey would grow up and have entire, lived lives. It isn't that I thought that they would die, so much as that they would just fade away, growing less distinct with time, and one day be no more. And here Davey is, as big as all religion, walking room to room in all his priestly pleasure causing me to wonder can it be that everyone I ever knew went on to have a whole life after I stopped knowing them. I would need a full year by the calendar to sit and devise fantasies of the particulars of that.

"Julie Ann's jerk of a husband never works; he's been in jail three times."

"Oh my." I feel so guilty. Julie Ann and I were friends, real friends right up till junior high, when I got put in all the smart kid classes. Me and Davey. I should have kept better track of her. I could have told her to break up the first time she went out with the bad husband. What am I saying? Davey could have had her and the five kids come live with him and grow up here.

"Is she Catholic too?" I say.

"No."

"How about your mother?"

"She's not Catholic either."

"No, I mean is she still here?"

"No, she moved with some guy to Florida the year that I converted. She never budged off the sofa all the years that we were growing up, and then we graduated and she moved a thousand miles away. She said she wouldn't be able to hold her head up when she went to the BY-LO for groceries, that everybody and his brother would know she was the mother of a full-blown priest with my long black robes billowing out behind my fat bum as I walked down the street. She said she could no longer show her face in town; she'd have to find a new church somewhere else where no one knew her."

Frankly, I'm impressed she had the energy to say all that.

Then suddenly I realize that Davey and I are no longer alone. In the dim light, I can just make out that invalid, in-validated mother of his over in the corner lying on the an-tique, horsehair sofa, underneath the gleaming crucifix. She has, she tells us in the voice that I remember, devoted the entire month of December to one single headache. She does not even open up her eyes to speak. But it's not just this mother who has now appeared. I look through the shadows, and there sits Julie Ann, a young girl, perched on the edge of a straight backed chair, wearing a blue dress, her hair in dreadful curls that she is just young and pretty enough to carry off. And there is a small child over in the corner sitting on the bare floor; she is crying softly with no sound, and Julie Ann walks over and lifts her gently in her arms, and the baby's features seem to change. I realize it is my little sister Annie and she is not dead at all.

And a boy—is it Davey?—runs in out of breath. Why, he is beautiful, with ruddy cheeks and curly hair and wiry limbs, a scratchy voice.

"They're coming," he says. "They're almost here."

And Julie Ann sits up very straight. The baby in her arms blinks, but sits stock still.

"They're coming," I say, and I seem to understand. My mother and my father stand now in the doorway, arm in arm. I seldom saw my father, not in real life, but he looks like the pictures taken when he and my mother were courting. He is tall, his eyes are bright.

"It's time," my mother says.

"They are almost here," my father whispers in her ear.

A man appears in the doorway. He looks like he just won a race.

"Am I too late?" he says.

"No, you're just right," the young boy Davey says and takes his hand and leads him to a chair, then sits down on his knee.

And there are other people now: my one grandma and my second one, the old lady with the Chex party mix who lived next door when I was growing up. The room is filling up, but none of this will be a problem. You can easily see the room could hold a thousand people. Davey's mother sleeps on. (You have to open up your eyes if you want to see the light. That's the deal.)

Here comes our preacher, the Reverend Lithgow, in his shiny, black suit flocked by all the children all across the years he buried in the ground, he, baffled-looking, shy and pleased, as though he'd been expecting something very like this.

It seems it's all to be brand new. I always used to pray that God would give us all do-overs, but I think I've always known that's not what mercy is.

Just then, Julie Ann's five children parade in, followed by their own children, and their children's children, six or seven generations, and a boy who will grow up to be the man that Julie Ann did one day marry. She catches my eye and motions to the doorway.

"That's your grandson there," she says as though I couldn't recognize my own, as though it could matter now I never had a child, not one in my whole lifetime. He has my nose, my finest feature.

You would have thought that someone might have mentioned that the soft breeze on the resurrection morning would feel just like the air that California redwoods make.

The room's become the largest meadow in the world. The earth shakes, just the slightest bit, like it is taking in a breath.

And then the trumpets sound.

"I guess it's not like what you thought." Davey and I are standing in the library. I'm putting on my coat. "The rectory, I mean."

"Oh no," I say. "It's wonderful. It's better than I ever dreamed."

"You probably think it's terrible that I became a priest," he says.

"Oh no, I think it's wonderful. I do. And Jesus does too."

"You think?" he says.

"I know," I say.

Five minutes more, and I am back out standing on the street. When I left, Davey headed back toward the dining room. I guess it is his suppertime.

I stand here on the sidewalk. The wind whips at the pavement grit and sand, but I'm not cold. In the rectory, in the room I calculate to be the library, some Irish/Italian woman—who in this light looks more Scandinavian than anything—turns on the table lamp. I stand and watch as one by one the lights go on in all the yellow table lamps in all the rooms. Was she, like me, one time a child who stood outside at night when it was cold?

I start to walk away, a little puzzled maybe, not quite certain. Did I see Davey Thomas come out on the porch tonight to get the newspaper, and did he ask me in, and be the priest, and tell me all about his mother and Julie Ann and her sorry excuse for a husband, or did I just imagine it? Did Davey really walk me room to room, remembering with me? Did all the people in the history of the world stand out on that mountain, waiting, ready there?

I do not think I could have made that last part up.

FINAL DISPOSITIONS

MY FAMILY IS DECIDING WHAT TO DO WITH ME. I am the oldest sibling. Always have been. I thought the years might mute the effect of that, but nothing so far. I have been, and I remain, the reason why the siblings take each new birthday with some measure of aplomb. *Well, I'm still four, seven, fourteen years younger than her.* My age, their comfort.

They hold disposition meetings. I am not invited, but I read the minutes of the meetings in the awkward silences and the odd questions during the phone calls that follow each conclave. "*How do you feel about Texas?*" "*Do you mind the cold?*" "*Do you have any special friend who lives in a big house? With a trained nurse?*"

I don't mind this actually. I am quite pleased at their level of involvement. There were decades when I think that they forgot I was alive, or if they remembered, they forgot I was their sister—or sister-in-law, a friendlier affiliation by a mile.

"Invite me to the meetings," I say to my brother Ned. "I promise not to voice opinions or spill brown liquid anywhere it will show. I'd like to know just what sort of thing might be under consideration."

"No," he says.

I like his style. The others would have said *What meet-ings*?

Ned got whatever integrity was floating in our gene pool.

"I might be able to help," I say, encouraged by his candor.

"I don't think so," Ned says.

"Are you sure you've saved no money whatsoever?" This would be my sister Irene—I mean Eileen—on the phone. I like it that I can never keep her name straight. It gives me hope.

"Zero money?" she says.

"Oh no," I say, "I saved a bundle. It's. Just. That. I. Spent. It. All."

Each word seems worthy of it's own personal sentence.

"Tom is coming over Tuesday morning. Please write that down. I'll wait," Eileen says. She pauses. I mime writing "Tooooosday, Doomsday," on the palm of my hand. "Tom's taking you for a ride."

"I'll be ready," I say. "Don't tell me what time. I like to be surprised."

"Ten o'clock. Wear stockings, Margaret," she says. "Wear shoes."

"Okey-doke," I say. "Okey-dokey."

People think that *crazy* is achieved when one day the gale force wind makes one final violent tear and your little craft slips its mooring. Oh no, it is achieved by you, who one knot at a time untie the tethers, whimsically at first, and then to some—or sometimes no—known purpose. You write a shameless letter to a friend who has blown you off once and for all time and say with no shame, "Why don't you like me? Did you ever?" You offer up the tidbits that will be the stuff of ridicule for certain, you pass them out to members of your family on a tray like some peculiar, worrisome hors d'oeuvres.

Eileen's husband Tom rings the doorbell. My siblings would have done the same. To walk right in would signal an affinity they neither feel nor seek.

"Would you like any sort of carbohydrate?" I ask. He is still standing on the porch. He never comes in unless it is a national holiday, and then it must be one celebrated across the board, not just by Jews or Christians or the tree people.

"I'm good," Tom says.

"I have no doubt," I say, "but are you hungry?"

"Oh . . ." The question catches him off guard. He clearly doesn't know the answer. It is one most often decided for him by Eileen.

"Why did you marry her?" I say.

"Who?" He is still busy with the last question.

"Oh yes," I say. "I had forgotten. You were married once before Eileen."

"I wasn't thinking about that," he says, rather simple, even for him.

"No," I say. "I wasn't thinking of her either. You never talk about her."

"Well, we should be on our way."

"Maybe I could go live with her, your first wife. Let's see, I'd be the sister-in-law of her ex-husband," I say. "Stranger things happen every day. A lot of them to me."

"Do you want a coat?" Tom says.

"No," I say. "I've got a closet full of them. But thanks."

He gives me a frightened stare. The man would not know humor if it wore a name tag.

"Well," he says, clearly with no heart whatsoever for the project. "We should be on our way."

He is so dutiful it makes his skin sag.

"Why are you doing this? Tom, this is your life. You could be dead by nightfall. A lot of people will be, and you could be one of them as easy as the next person. Let's forget about wherever Eileen wants you to take me. It will only be a waste of time. They won't admit me. It will turn out they only take retired Presbyterian clergy. Or, Ned won't want to pay for it. Or, they'll have a waiting list. Or, at the last minute I'll kick the bucket. If this is the last day of your life, trust me when I tell you, you will want to have spent it some other way no matter if you end up in hell or heaven."

"I don't believe in hell."

"Well, there you go."

It's the first nearly interesting thing I've heard him say since he met my sister.

"What was she like?" I say.

"Who?"

"Wife One. Eileen's predecessor."

"I don't remember." Tom says. "I've been married to Eileen for nearly thirty years."

"I'm sorry," I say. I am, too. I always thought he was born this way, never thinking what it might do to a person to be married to Eileen.

"Why did you marry her?" I say.

"Oh, I was young." He makes it sound a rather unusual thing to be. "I was young. And she was beautiful."

"Eileen?"

"Janet Moyer." His voice is just about a whisper. "Janet Helen Moyer. Look, we really need to go. Eileen has made an appointment for you."

My sister is forever and a day making things for people: appointments and decoupage, Rice Krispies treats and bright fabric snakes you're meant to keep your plastic bag collection in.

I grab my pocketbook and slam the door behind me.

"You want to lock that?" Tom says.

"I do not," I say.

It takes me fourteen minutes to locate Janet Helen Moyer on Google. First I typed in "ex-wives." Four million, one hundred and six results. Then I tried her name, which reduces that number by about four million. Turns out she illustrates books for dyslexic children, using words as illustration. She calls them "word pictures."

It seems she draws words under the pseudonym of Janelle Roy—not the most profligate use of the imagination, but I allow for the possibility that she makes the most of what's she's got, a habit I refuse to despise. I send her off an e-mail through her website to say my six-year-old dyslexic son, Leroy, reads her illustrations with great pleasure as does his auntie Eileen Ferguson (just in case Janelle Roy is a woman given to putting two and two together).

I issue myself a poetic license: I do not have a son named Leroy, or any other name, but if I let my childlessness figure largely in every single e-mail I send off, I might as well downgrade to dial-up and be done with it.

Janelle Roy (aka Wife One) sends an e-mail in return. She wishes me "every joy"—which strikes me as being a bit over the top, but I prefer it to a curse, and let it be. The large print at the bottom of the e-mail says that she will be giving a reading of her words at "a mall near you." That is to say, near me. I click on the bar that says, *Find a Mall near you,* hardly troubling to fret that Mall is capitalized, only to find the Mall (maul?) is even nearer than I thought.

I call Eileen to arrange a little rendezvous with her hubby's previous wife. Stir the pot a bit. The answering machine picks up. Eileen hasn't answered her phone since that little fiasco the day Tom took me to the perpetual care place. How was I to know she'd paid a hundred and forty bucks for the evaluation? How was I to know she'd sent me there to take a test? A person should be told these things. Now she's terrified no place will have me—as though I'd want to go to any place where people were excluded on the basis of how strenuously they agreed or disagreed with statements like "I am not worried about the future."

I leave a message for Eileen. "There is an author reading from a book, *The Idiot's Guide to Nursing Homes,*" I say. "Tuesday night at seven at the mall in Pittsfield. Could you drive me? I could take the bus, but I didn't know if you wanted me appearing in public unchaperoned. Plus, if the bus crashed and I didn't get killed, but only severely maimed and injured, we'd be worse off than we already are."

Eileen picks up just as I am finishing the final phrase.

"Hello," she says.

"Hello," I say.

"Who is this?" she says.

"Who is this?" I say.

And we're off to the races.

Eileen drops me at the main entrance to the mall. I allow it. I really can't walk as well when I am with her.

There's an old man standing by the door with a collection can, yellow, labeled in bright red, FOR THE RETARDED, which I take to mean he's working freelance. The organized prefer "developmentally disabled." I don't know. *Retarded* seems more hopeful some way. It's nothing permanent or cast in stone, but more a matter of speed than anything. Timing. "Her progress is only retarded, slowed a bit, delayed, but coming—oh yes coming certainly. Just not today." *Retarded* gives a person something to look forward to.

"Well, I must say that was a good evening." When Eileen found out I'd read the listing wrong, her sincere pleasure at my having made a mistake was enough to sweeten the whole night.

Eileen and I are shut back up inside the brand-new Japanese container that we will travel home in—or if not, that will transport us to our *long home.*

"Long home." I say the words out loud. They sound portentous as we drive off together into the black night. "Have you ever heard the phrase 'long home,' referring to death—or, I guess, to where death takes us to?"

"Don't talk about death," Eileen says. "It's morbid."

"Duh," I say, the word *duh* being one of the three innovations of the last half century that are really worth something, the other two being e-mail and breakfast all day at fast-food restaurants. I don't go to fast-food restaurants, but I like knowing if I did I could get a fried-egg sandwich in the middle of the afternoon.

"I don't know why you have to work death into every conversation," Eileen says. "Don't think I didn't hear you mention it to that woman tonight, the one with those oxygen tubes in her nose."

"The way she looked, it seems to me it would have been impolite *not* to mention death. And don't say you didn't sense the general amazement that she was still alive when we went to get our coats. Trust me, death's on everybody's mind, at least four times a day."

"Not mine," Eileen says. "I concentrate on happy things, like the nice books that lady was showing tonight. Her word pictures were beautiful."

I wonder would she be calling Janelle Moy, aka Janet Helen Moyer, a "lady" if she knew the author was the one woman in the universe she'd shared a husband with.

"What did you think of her?" I say.

"I thought that if she needed oxygen, perhaps she might be more comfortable at home than in a bookstore."

"I didn't mean her," I say. "I meant, what did you think of the author?"

"Some day you will appreciate what I am trying to do for you, Margaret."

"Don't hold your breath," I say. "Get it, it's an oxygen-tank joke. But what did you think of the author?"

"Why do you care?"

"Because she was Tom's wife."

Damn. I wasn't going to tell Eileen that—or, at least not until we had invited Janet Helen Royer to Thanksgiving. See, this is why I am no earthly good at card games. I cannot keep a secret for two minutes in a row.

"Tom who?"

She's asking for form's sake. She knows *Tom who.*

"Your Tom."

"But Tom's first wife's name was Janet, this woman was Janelle."

"Uh, that's not exactly DNA evidence."

"You knew it was her. You brought me on purpose. You told me it was a book on nursing homes."

"Eileen, what person in their right mind would drive twenty-five miles on a school night to get the author to sign a book on nursing homes."

"I'm gonna' tell," Eileen says and suddenly she is four, and I am eight, and neither one of us has even heard of Alzheimer's or knee replacements or long-term care insurance. The only thing in fact we know of human tragedy is what goes on inside our family.

"Who you gonna tell?" I say, but already I am warming to the prospect of our reporting all the crimes committed on the planet to the proper authorities. I want to take Eileen by her thin, clammy hand, her diamonds hurting both our fingers in the tightness of the grip. I want to pull her out of the car and drag her down the street for blocks, calling out to strangers on the way, *Police station! Where is the police station! Is that it?* and pull her with me through the heavy doors and grab the sleeve of the first policeman that we see and say, *Come quick. I need you to arrest our parents. They are scaring us to death, and when we are old women we will put each other into nursing homes and into unnatural situations in bookstores in shopping malls. Malls. Places where people go so they won't have to think about death. Oh never mind! Just come. You need to lock them up and throw away the key.*

"Remember," I say to Eileen, in a voice gone hoarse from all the yelling that I should have done a half century ago, "remember the night you started to take Ned downtown to the police station, to show them the belt-buckle welts, the places where the tip end broke the skin?"

"Oh Margaret. That was in another lifetime."

"No. No, it wasn't. It was this same lifetime. This same one we're living in tonight. There is only just the one."

"Well," Eileen says. "I never got there. I met Grandma Chase at the corner, and I told her where I was taking him, and she told me to go back home and to never, ever tell a living soul, or God would punish me."

A different God from that crawls into the backseat as we stop for the light.

"I was just trying to help," Eileen says. "I was just trying to do the right thing, with Ned. I was just trying to save his life."

Tell her she did. It's God, in the backseat.

"You tell her," I say to Him.

Nah. She's gotta hear it from you, He whispers in a raspy, smoker's voice.

"You did save Ned's life," I say.

God clears His throat, and makes a "Go on" motion with his hand.

"I mean, look at him," I say. "Look at Ned's marriage. Look at his kids. Look at their kids. He's had practically the best life I know."

"Yeah, well."

"Yeah, well, why do you think that is?"

"Well…."

"Hello? Because of you."

I know she gets it. When a thing is true, you don't have to explain. I turn around to wink at God, but He's gone. Off to save some other sisters. It must take Him all night just to do one neighborhood.

"And I *am* just trying to help you," Eileen says.

"I know," I say. "And I was just trying to help you, taking you to meet old Janet Moyer tonight at the bookstore."

"No, you weren't," Eileen says as she pulls into my driveway, a little closer to the holly bushes than she might have liked.

"No, I wasn't," I say.

I open the car door.

"Did you forgive them?" I say. "The parents. For what they did."

"Yup," Eileen says. "I did."

She gets out and walks around the car.

"And do you forgive me?" I say.

"Nope," she says, and she takes my hand and pulls just hard enough to make my standing up a thing that I can do, then lets me lean, pretty hard at first, on her arm as we go up the walk. "Not in this or any other lifetime," she says.

There's a priest in my kitchen. If I had to go to church to confess my sins, I'd spend my whole life in the car driving there and back and wouldn't need a nursing home or any other housing.

No matter that my priest is one I have concocted out of equal parts of worn, black, shiny cloth and blessed fathers born on the silver screen, he is just as unforgiving as the real thing. Forget the fact that I have purged the fey Bing Crosby; long lines of priests in handcuffs on the evening news; fabled fathers that my Catholic friends curse after they have lost their faith or seriously misplaced it; still, mine is no more efficacious than the fat man who waddles to the altar at St. Michael's every morning, even government holidays.

Still, he is my confessor. There are agents in our lives we do not choose.

"Forgive me, Father, for I have sinned," I mumble as I open up the freezer and take out a bag of frozen cherries. "It has been three hours since my last confession."

He's silent as the night.

I wait him out.

"OK, OK," he says, "what did you do this time?"

I keep him on retainer for the reason that he has less patience than I do.

"I took my sister to a bookstore for the express purpose of cutting her down to size. Or, at the very least, of annoying the hell out of her."

"And did it work?"

"Nah. Hardly."

"So you are guilty of the sin of wasting time created by the Eternal One."

"That too."

"Are you sorry?"

"Sort of. I wish she had gotten really angry and thrown her purse at my head and forced me out of the car by the side of the road on a dark and stormy night, the avenue awash in burglars and other men in urgent need of immediate incarceration."

"*You can't always get what you want.*" He sings it. He is a priest who, if he ever moved beyond the walls of this my kitchen, would play guitar in church and have the Host be sourdough. "You want to be punished for your sins," he says. "There is no penance in the book for sins against the sister. And so there can be no forgiveness."

"Eileen just told me that tonight."

"And she, an atheist," he says, "a card-carrying member of the club that says that sin is only mental illness, mental flu, mental TB, mental appendicitis."

"But we know better."

"We know *worse*," he says. "Sin's the best hope we've got. If it's mental, all we've got is pills, and they stop working the day that you stop taking them. Ah, but sin…." His voice softens. "Sin can be named and napalmed. You gotta love a God who's up to that. Your problem is you always want to save yourself."

It's a sermon that I've heard before.

"So, what would you say to giving me a few Hail Marys here?"

"All they do is keep you busy. They only sandblast sloth. What we need here is a Savior."

He shakes his head, and for the first time I notice that his hair falls in gentle waves onto his shoulders.

"I always thought that you were bald," I say.

"I'm not," he says. "You never really look at me."

"I never really look at anyone. Could I offer you a cherry?" I hold out the bag.

"They're frozen," he says and grabs the bag of designer potato chips from the bread box and sits down at the table to read the paper.

I don't know what the priest in your kitchen is like. Mine is a slave to carbohydrates.

I take my glasses off and move my face six inches from the mirror on the wall. My eyebrow is a composite of so many sorts of strands. I am absorbed. Time stops for my eyebrow inspection, as time will if ever you are lost inside a moment. Time stops and waits, and then you look away, and time starts up again.

That's how I come to know there is eternity.

I'm lying on the floor. And in this slim interval between bemusement and the stark desperation I am planning, the room has become all ceiling. It is wider than the floor, and the room is one of those odd shapes you study in geometry but never come across in your real life. There's lots of real life on the floor.

The underbelly of the antique, carved desk my grandmother wrote her grocery-shopping list upon is nothing more than what appears to be a piece of Masonite. And exactly where have I pulled that mid-century word from? I take no small amount of comfort from its having come to me so easily. I do not think a person calls back the word *Masonite* if she has had a stroke.

I take it also as proof definitive I have not lost my mind. I give myself these periodic evaluations. A person likes to know just where she stands—or in my case, lies. I will assume I have not hurt my head. I find out some extent of the damage, though, when I try to drag me, soul and body—one so thin, the other so heavy—across the kitchen floor. I left the telephone up on the kitchen counter when I immigrated to the floor, and now they're telling me it is a one-way trip I've taken.

The light has moved from the front porch to the back deck when I awaken next. Cold. I'm mostly cold. And I am sad and clutch the sadness like an old baby blanket I've uncovered in a bureau drawer. It's faded, ragged, aged by time and overuse, but it is there; that's the main thing. If I am sad, if sad is something I can still be, then it will be all right.

Sometime later I open my eyes, and it is dark. But darkness happens, it occurs to me, once every day.

The next time I awaken, Eileen is beside me with a magazine. She's sitting in a chair. Her make-up isn't working for her. Any shade of orange will just betray you in the end. The floor I'm lying on has gone all soft and white and warm, and I am loving lying here.

"I was sad," I tell Eileen. "I was cold, but I was sad."

"Oh, Margaret. You're awake. We were so worried. How do you feel?"

"Fine," I say. "Nice and warm." I don't say it, but the sadness is all gone. Now I will have to see just how I am to live with that.

"Life is so short these days."

The words are whispered in a voice I do not recognize, out in the hallway, whispered by a person I don't know— although, it would probably be good for me to spend some time with a person who says such things without a twisted curl, a single saffron thread, of irony.

Irony is mother's milk to me, but at the end of the day it doesn't make a twiggy twig of difference. It's not how you view your life; it's what happens in your life that matters.

Right now, what's happened to me matters a great deal. I have a heart that let me down, as I have long suspected it might one day do. It actually stopped beating. Tell that to the lady in customer service when you go to get my money back.

And when that happens to your heart and you live to tell the story, people demand it be a good one. Even strangers in blue-spotted nightgowns sliding down the hallways, holding on for dear life to some rolling pole, transparent plastic bags in full sway, asses veiled from public view by the strength of loosely knotted ties—even they arrest their snail-creep, stop the rolling poles, and say in voices manufactured down in intubated airways, "What was it like?"

I tell them what they want to hear, once they have told me precisely what that is. They are not shy about requests. Then it's just a matter of a spattering of *yeses* and the odd *no*, and a great deal of shaking of the head.

"Did you see a great white light?"

"Why, yes I did."

"And was it the brightest thing you ever saw or hope to see?"

"It was," I say.

"Were you amazed?"

"Why, I still am."

"Is there hell then?" A former Christian missionary, who has come to write her final chapter as a nurse, asks me this while standing at the trash chute to the incinerator. "Is there hell?" she says.

"Oh yes," I say.

"I thought so." She upends her schoolroom metal basket, sending something that sounds like a bowling ball with spikes on it crashing down the chute. "I thought so," she says. "But you never know."

"No," I say. "You never do."

Actually, though, I do know. I have seen what does await us. The whole thing. There is good reason that we are not told. There is good reason why we cannot tell what we have seen and why the white light is so popular in stories resurrected people tell. White, the color of no story. Blinding-light transparency, the opposite of truth.

Everybody asks what is it like, everybody but Eileen. Her, I would tell.

My new home is a kennel. No matter that every dog in the whole place is registered and has had all its shots. I call it the "kennel club." It drives Eileen nuts.

"They give us dog food for lunch," I tell her. "In dog dishes. With dog silverware."

"Oh, Margaret, stop it. They've got paella on the menu for tonight."

"Don't let them fool you. That's code for mussel shells in red food coloring broth. Woof, woof," I bark.

Eileen sets about tidying up the room, which she keeps tidied up to within an inch of its life.

"Eileen," I say. "Sit down. Stop fidgeting. Take a pill. Read a book. I have a copy of *Great Dog Expectations* I got from the pound library."

She doesn't take the bait. She knows me well enough to know that in another fifteen seconds I will be so sick of dog jokes I'll never bark again.

"It is awful," I tell her. "Here," I say, in case there's any question just where *awful* is.

I've not felt sad one moment since they brought me here the day I left the hospital.

Eileen comes to visit dutifully—far more often than I'd visit her, I'm pretty sure.

I have a dream, and in the dream I am in kindergarten, and Eileen is my grandfather. And every day she walks me to the school and sits outside the schoolhouse door on an old wooden, backless bench, sits there until school is over, and then she walks me home. I wake up feeling as safe as that. But sad, not safe, is what I want to feel. Safe means there's harm and danger out there, just on the other side of that thin windowpane. But sad—sad means there is love, to be missed or had, and lost and maybe had again, or if not, at least to be longed for, missed and reminisced about and carried in you in a place where safe has never been. Sad is the deep of feeling. Sad tells a person that good is.

And here I am, arrived at the asylum, I, who always thought that safe was everything, and only now the telegram bearing this insight as new information gets forwarded to this address, carried by the last deliveryman on earth, on the day before the world ends.

Eileen wants me to sign a power of attorney: a sheaf of papers to declare that she can forge my signature on anything she wants and never spend a single night in jail.

"No," I say. That's the long answer. The shorter answer is the silent one. The terse refusal is my faking palsied hands. I lift my paws, gone claw-like in pantomime, let one side of my mouth droop, my eyes bug out, and stare.

"It isn't funny," Eileen says.

"Aren't you enjoying this?" I say.

She scowls.

"No," I say. "I'm serious. I honestly hope that you are getting something from the roles we have been cast in here. You are well and strong and truly married, and I am enfeebled in this frightful way, and I just hope you feel the muscles of that victory. Living well, that best revenge."

"I'm not looking for revenge," she says. Her shoulders slump, and I would write a check with lots of zeros on the money line if she could be all spit and vinegar again, the little, bony girl, all fire and spine, who told our brother he could fly if he jumped off of the armoire, who said ice cream would come from the light socket if you wet you finger and put it in the hole; that girl I begged our father to beat one Sunday afternoon for her nefarious infractions, and when, finally near nightfall, he did, the girl I imagined strong enough to turn on him and slay him. We had a King James English childhood with verbs that could rear up on their hind legs and scare tall men. I want Eileen to be as powerful as she seemed then. As mean.

"You want revenge," I say.

"No, Margaret, I don't," she says. "I'm too tired for revenge. You want revenge."

"No, I don't," I say, telling us both a thing we didn't know.

"Do you think that we will ever be friends?" I say. "You and me."

"We're sisters," Eileen says.

I know she's right.

We could be friends—if you would change every single thing about you, I don't say to her; she doesn't say to me.

We sit pretending it were possible if only the wanting were there, when we both know that we will not be friends until we find ourselves on the Last Day, discovered and forgiven.

I'm pretending I am dead. It makes a change. There are few amusements left to me. I've tired of magazines. I lie, not breathing, on the bed, mouth gaping, eyes staring. Until I blink. It's probably just as well I never took up acting.

The matron enters on her clicky shoes. I call her "the matron" in my mind, like some housemistress shrew whom Dickens dissed—or would have if he'd thought of it.

"And we are how this morning?" the dragon lady says.

I don't answer. I'm pretending she is dead.

"Cat's got our tongue?" she says.

I see this boiled tongue we were just about to slice and serve with serious mustard and a sturdy stein of Old Peculiar Beer, then see it being pounced on by an enormous tabby who, fierce fat feline though she be, can do little more than gnaw one corner.

"Eeeewww," I say involuntarily.

"Do we have a problem?"

"Any number I should think," I say. *I'm old and you're mean, for starters.* I don't say it. I'm a big fan of the obvious speaking for itself.

"Well, we will take care of you."

A threat if I ever heard one.

Eileen peeks her head around the door frame. Have I ever been so glad of her appearance?

"May I come in?" Eileen says.

"No," the matron says, more brusquely than even she might have chosen. "No, I'll come out. If you don't mind, I'd like to have a word with you. We don't mind, do we?" she says to me.

I lie back, pretend to be dead. No one appears to notice or to care.

"We will be moving her today." The matron's voice carries from the corridor, as she must surely know it would. Her voice is noisy, like her shoes. She must have been an irritating child.

"Moving?" Eileen says.

"Yes, dear. It's time. We must accept these things."

Who's this "we," white man? As Tonto said to the Lone Ranger when the Comanches appear.

"Moving where?" Eileen's staying focused here. I like that.

"Upstairs, dear. To the Sunshine Unit." Good grief, we're back to second grade, when everybody knew that "Bluebirds" was a euphemism for the kids who'd probably never learn to read.

"But my understanding is that the higher floors are for people with bigger problems?" Eileen can sling euphemisms with the best of them. "Margaret's mind is clear as it ever was."

"Dear, she's incontinent."

Shit! I didn't want Eileen to know. I did not want Eileen to know. I so wanted her not to know.

"A secretary that I work with is incontinent." Eileen's voice is matter-of-fact. I had forgotten she looks at life with a less impassioned eye than her incontinent sister.

No matter. I hate to have her know. To have her thinking of that every time she looks at me. *She pees herself,* our mother would have said, whispering derision.

"Dear, we have to accept that there will be more changes."

"My name is Mrs. Ferguson," Eileen says.

You go, girl!

"Well, Mrs. Ferguson, dear, we need to accept little changes along the way."

Little changes. They're shipping me to hell.

"She's fine right here," Eileen says.

"And she will be fine upstairs, dear."

"Well, she won't be going upstairs," Eileen says.

"Dear, you have no choice."

"Actually," Eileen says. "I do. We have decided that my sister will be leaving Pine Brook."

"And where will you put her, dear?"

"We will not *put her* anywhere. She will be coming home to live with me. We have been planning this for quite some time."

Hallelujah! I feel a sweet and certain sadness start up at the bottom of my toes and fill up all of me. Sadness everywhere. Sadness I have sought in every hiding place.

"Well, I think you will be surprised to learn just how difficult your sister can be."

"I will not be surprised at all. It's a thing I knew about before you were born."

Cue the angels. Blow the pitch pipe.

Eileen appears around the corner. She's one determined Girl Scout. "Let's pack your things, Margaret. We're getting out of here."

"Whatever you say, Sparky."

Eileen carries a small overnight bag filled with what I need tonight.

"We'll be back for all her things later," she tells the matron, who is standing at the front door, trying to look as though her life has meaning.

Eileen takes me by the hand and drags me past the woman, and there is no grandmother on the planet earth who will stop her this afternoon, no force in hell or heaven that would dare try.

"Well, good luck, dear," the matron says as we pass by.

"My name is Mrs. Ferguson," Eileen says, icy, stern.

"So, should I call you that too?" I say and squeeze her hand as she all but drags me across the parking lot.

When Eileen's grandson was very young, I took him to the movies, and the only movie not sold out that afternoon was *The Madness of King George*. Driving home that day, I asked the little boy if he had understood the movie. "Sure," he said. "The people said, 'God save the King,' and at the end of the movie, God did."

"Mrs. Ferguson," I say as Eileen climbs into the driver's seat and buckles in. "I like the way this ends. I like what this ending does to the whole story."

"Don't call me Mrs. Ferguson."

Eileen puts her foot down and the car jerks forward. The whole way home she pumps the gas pedal, up and down. It's how she drives, it's how she's always driven. But tonight I think she'll get us where we need to go.

ABOUT THE AUTHOR

Linda McCullough Moore is the author of the literary novel, *The Distance Between*, and more than 200 shorter works of fiction, essay, memoir and poetry, published in such places as *The Massachusetts Review, The Sun, The Alaska Quarterly Review, Queen's Quarterly, Glimmer Train, House Beautiful, The Boston Globe,* and *The Southern Review.* She is the winner and finalist for a number of short fiction awards, including *The Pushcart Prize XXXV.* She lives in Northampton, Massachusetts, where for the past two decades she has taught weekly creative writing workshops and mentored aspiring writers.

ACKNOWLEDGMENTS

The ones who receive our work, who truly take it in, are the ones who made it possible. I couldn't have written these stories were it not for the stories of Alice Munro.

I couldn't have written these stories were it not for William Trevor, Maeve Brennan, Marilynne Robinson, or a host of other writers, not to mention the debt I owe to the pulsing cadence of the language in the King James English Bible, to the words and stories of my father. And I couldn't have written these stories without a troop of believers: Missy, Brett, Carol, Pat, Nancy, Jean, Sarah, Penny, Maggie, and so very many others. You know who you are, but may never know how much you mean to me.

I give thanks to Ronald Spatz and Sy Safransky and Andrew Snee and Melanie Fleishman and John Wilson, editors with heart and wisdom. To Steve Strimer, the founder of the feast, the wisest and most patient of men. His talent and kindness, a rare blessing. And to Jim Shinnick, for such generosity and craft.

Finally, to Asa. To Judd and Katie. To Gideon. The loves of my life.

And to my God, from whom all blessings flow.